FLUFFY'S REVOLUTION

TED MYERS

Black Rose Writing | Texas

ISBN: 978-1-68433-231-1
PUBLISHED BY BLACK ROSE WRITING
www.blackrosewriting.com

Printed in the United States of America
Suggested Retail Price (SRP) $15.95

Fluffy's Revolution is printed in Chaparral Pro
© 2019 Author Photo by Janet Caliri
Cover Design by Delbar Tourminaei (TRIXMEDIA Inc.)

To Alex, Lora, Brad, and Lily Moon.

In memory of Ron DeZure (1939-2018), Jaiananda, and Rocky

Special Thanks to Ron and Deborah for the readthrough and feedback

FLUFFY'S REVOLUTION

CHAPTER ONE — WELCOME TO THE WORLD

Fluffy was furious. Her tail bristled and twitched as she paced up and back on the professor's long desk. Above the desk the big screen showed a web page with a news article: 10,000 GAB PETS EUTHANIZED IN MUMBAI. "Euthanized? *Euthanized?* Why don't they call it what it is?" said Fluffy, "Murder, clear and simple." Her voice emanated from the computer speakers, even as her words unfurled across the bottom of the screen like a news crawl.

Lately, Fluffy had been surfing the web every day, reading article after article about the efforts of humans to eradicate GAB (Genetically Altered Brain) animals and diatribes written by animal revolutionaries advocating a GAB uprising.

The professor looked at the article and shook his head sadly. "They're doing the same thing here," he said, "but Epps controls the media, so we don't hear about it."

"There's a big demonstration in Haines Park tomorrow. Can we go, Dad?"

"No," said the professor. "It's just what Epps and his thug cops want: an excuse to beat and arrest more people and animals. Don't you see, Fluffy? Government by the corporations is failing. The Triumvirate needs this trumped-up terrorist scare to distract the public. The GABs are a great target because they're not human. There's been no terrorism. They haven't done anything beyond rhetoric, some vandalism and theft, and a few protests."

"Well, maybe we should," said Fluffy. "Maybe our only hope is to rise up against the human oppressors and fight for our rights."

Fluffy was an exceptionally intelligent feline, even by 2135 standards. She had a lovely white face that peaked in a star in the center of her forehead. The rest of her was mostly gray-and-black tabby, but her chest, paws, and underbelly were pure white. She had long, thick fur, a bushy tail, and inquisitive green eyes that were outlined in black as if she were wearing eye makeup.

Professor James Riordan, the human Fluffy called Dad, was a once-handsome, graying man about sixty with rheumy blue eyes and a ruddy complexion.

"Humans are scum, Fluffy. Make no mistake about that," said the professor. "But don't try to match them in violence; no other species on the planet is as vicious. Don't try to beat humans at their game; make them play yours."

"But what is our game, Dad? I don't want bloodshed, but the humans are killing my fellow GABs by the thousands. And what about all the human supporters? We don't even know what's happening to them. I can't just sit by and watch."

"GABs have unique skills," said the professor. "Hone them, make yourself invaluable to humans with your powers of telepathy and telekinesis."

It was only four o'clock in the afternoon and the professor was already in his cups. He had his reasons for drinking and being bitter. Once a prominent and respected writer and the most popular teacher in the English Department at Kingston University, he had resigned in disgrace when his colleagues, solely out of envy for his dynamic and innovative teaching methods and the love of his students, had set him up to be caught in a compromising position with a female student. They had hired the girl to entrap him, and to his eternal regret, he had gone for the bait.

It all started with the mouse brain experiments, way back in 2015, 120 years ago. Scientists had implanted elements of human DNA called enhancers into the brains of unborn mouse embryos. The resultant mice were born with brains that were twelve percent larger than the normal mouse brain. These new mice were called Genetically Altered Brain animals, or GABs. This and the many subsequent experiments were all done with the intention of learning more about the evolution of the human brain, and what made the human species evolve with a brain that was so superior to the rest of the animal kingdom. At the time, some people laughingly speculated that this might cause animal brains to become equal to human brains somewhere down the line. Scientists dismissed this as not being a possibility for thousands of years.

But something had happened. When they started enlarging the brains of domesticated animals—dogs, cats, and the occasional pig—and those animals mated and had offspring, the evolutionary process of their brains went haywire, and animal brains started evolving at a frightening rate, much the same as global warming had spun out of control in the late twenty-first century, and turned Kingston, New York into the largest seaport on the Eastern Seaboard.

Their bodies stayed the same as their brains evolved exponentially over the generations. To compensate for their physical limitations—such as the shape of their palates and tongues preventing them from speaking, and their lack of opposable thumbs preventing them from grasping or pulling a trigger—GAB animals gradually started to develop telepathic and telekinetic powers. At first, these expressed themselves as random acts of vandalism, such as moving valuable objects off their shelves and smashing them when they were displeased by their "masters." But now they had developed these abilities to enable them to open doors, feed themselves, and turn electronic devices on and off.

Humans, egged on by their corporate rulers, responded in a predictably human manner: with fear and hatred. They figured if these animals continued to proliferate while the human population was declining, they would soon take over and subjugate the humans, just as humans had done to animals for so many thousands of years. The Triumvirate, the troika of the world's most powerful corporations who ruled the planet, decided to round up and suppress the "troublemakers," outlawing animal access to computers, denouncing animal activists as terrorists. Ultimately, they instituted a worldwide policy of exterminating all GAB animals found without a human guardian.

When computers became thought-activated, the animals used it to blog, proclaiming their equality to humans and demanding their freedom. When voices became available, enabling GABs to speak out loud through computer speakers, Fluffy chose the voice of Katharine Hepburn, a film actress who had lived 200 years ago, because she sounded "defiant."

Fluffy and the professor lived in the fashionable Upper East Side of Kingston, on the 150th floor of a high-rise overlooking the Kingston harbor and the bay beyond. The professor's late wife, a woman of means from an old New York family, had bought the apartment, and the professor had inherited it when she died five years ago.

Since then, the professor had led a solitary life, and rarely interacted with other humans. And, at five years old, Fluffy had never interacted with anyone other than the professor. They had been each other's sole companion since she was a kitten. Every day he would continue her education, recommending books, which she read on her own small tablet: great literature, modern fiction, memoirs, biographies, and history. Neither of them was too keen on math or science, but Fluffy studied biology and genetics to learn the history of her kind. Today, about a third of all the mice, dogs and cats, and about an eighth of all the pigs on Earth were GABs.

At night when the computers went off, Fluffy and the professor reverted to the traditional non-verbal relationship between man and cat. Fluffy would spend long hours purring in his lap while he brushed the tangles out of her fur or petted her and stroked her head in just the right way. She loved it when he read her Shakespeare's sonnets, or her favorite poem—that one about the tiger by William Blake. But best of all were the movies. They both loved to watch the old movies made in the early twentieth century. The professor would run them before going to sleep. Fluffy would sit beside him on the bed and stare in fascination at these visions of an ancient black-and-white world, where people lived wildly, passionately, where cars and trucks and trains made loud noises, and where the only place animals spoke was in cartoons. When it was time to go to sleep, she would nuzzle up into the crook of his armpit and fall asleep breathing in that reassuring essence. To Fluffy, it was the smell of safety.

The next day, they watched the demonstration in the park on the big screen. Pro-animal rights people marched, carrying signs that said things like ALL BEINGS ARE EQUAL and STOP THE KILLING! And GAB animals marched without their tracking collars, levitating signs over their heads, that said things like IF I CAN DO THIS, I CAN LIVE FREE. Seeing animals do these things on TV scared the hell out of the ignorant masses. Soon, the riot cops arrived and turned the peaceful demonstration into a riot. They tear-gassed the crowd and rounded up as many protestors as they could catch. They stuffed them into big trucks, animals in some, humans in others, and carted them off to god knows where.

The professor turned off the screen and they sat in silence. At length, Fluffy spoke.

"I've been thinking a lot about Jack lately."

"Who?"

Fluffy looked at him. "My brother, Jack... the one you *didn't* take."

The professor looked sheepish. She was right, of course. He should have taken Jack, even though he thought they were just ordinary cats.

Five years earlier, the professor had purchased Fluffy in an open-air flea market from a dirty-faced little girl, a poor kid of about seven. She was huddled against a fence behind one of the stalls with a box of newly-weaned kittens. She had two left; both looked like little balls of fluff. Riordan thought he'd get one for his wife, who was bed-ridden with terrible headaches. "How much do you want for this one?" he asked, picking up Fluffy.

"Two dollars."

"Okay," said the professor, handing her the money. "I think I'll call her Athena, after the goddess of wisdom and heroism."

"It's *Fluffy*," insisted the little girl.

"Okay, Fluffy."

"You have to promise to keep it Fluffy or no sale. Promise?"

"I promise. What's the other one's name?"

"Jack. He's the runt of the litter. Nobody wants him."

"Too bad. Well, good luck, Jack," said the professor, giving the last little furball a pat on the head, and he left with Fluffy tucked into the pocket of his coat.

The professor's wife died of a brain hemorrhage a few days later, and Riordan channeled his grief into raising Fluffy as if she were his child. It wasn't long before he realized he had purchased a genuine GAB.

He got her a little red rubber ball to bat around. This amused her for about a day. After that, she would stare intently at the ball for days on end. Finally, she got it to roll around without touching it. A few days after that she got it to levitate off the ground. She quickly discovered that, when she let it go in midair, it would bounce, and the higher she lifted it, the higher it would bounce. Pretty soon, she was getting her kicks by bouncing the ball into the professor's soup during dinner.

So, the professor tried an experiment. He bought a coloring book with pictures of animals and a set of crayons. He took the crayons out of the box and colored in the first page for Fluffy—a lion. Then he left her alone with the book and the crayons. Within a day she was able to lift a crayon and make marks on the paper. By the second day, she could color inside the lines with one crayon. By the third day, she could color an entire page in different colors. From there, it progressed to learning her ABC's, reading, and ultimately writing. One day, the professor woke up and found a page from the coloring book on the floor. Fluffy had colored a picture of a cat. She made it look like her. Under it was a single word written in crude block letters in red crayon: JACK. Fluffy had written the name of her lost brother.

"I keep thinking Jack is calling out to me," said Fluffy. "Like he's in trouble of some kind." She had spoken of getting psychic communications from her brother for years, but the professor thought she was imagining it.

"Look, I'm sorry I didn't take Jack when I took you, alright? I made a mistake. In any case, there's nothing we can do to help Jack now."

Fluffy was silent. She just moped around the house and didn't speak for the next few days. She even stopped watching the old movies and slept on a chair in the living room. The professor was worried. At last, he insisted she tell him what was on her mind.

"I have to find my brother."

"Fluffy, you're not thinking of going out *there*?" The professor indicated the bustling city below.

"Yes, I have to. I know he needs me. And I want to find other GABs and join the resistance."

The professor stood up and threw up his hands in exasperation. "Fluffy, that's crazy. Your chances of survival are nil. With your experience of the world…"

"I'm going," she said.

He walked to the balcony and gazed down at the city. "Then I'll go with you."

"No, you'll just attract attention and get us both in trouble. No, I have to do this alone."

"Fluffy, you don't have any idea what it's like for an animal alone in the world. The Animal Control people are everywhere, scouring the streets for strays, sucking them up by the dozens, and taking them off to the extermination centers."

"I have to chance it, Dad. This is just something I have to do."

"But how do you expect to find him? There's a huge, crowded city out there."

"He will guide me to him."

The professor hung his head. He thought for a long moment. "I guess I can't stop you. You're all grown up now. So, when are you leaving?"

Fluffy looked at the floor. The last thing she wanted to do was hurt her dad, and she knew she was about to do it. "Now. Can you please take off my tracking collar?"

Every GAB animal was required to wear a collar which enabled Animal Control to see their exact location at any moment, anywhere in the world. The professor unclasped Fluffy's collar. He had tears in his eyes. "I'll move it around the house every day, so they think you're still here," he said. "Do you want me to take you down in the elevator?"

"No," said Fluffy. "I need to practice my telekinesis. Let me try to get out by myself."

Fluffy rubbed up against his leg, the equivalent of a hug. Riordan impulsively scooped her up, hugged her to his chest, kissed her on the head, then put her back down. She looked intently at the front door of the apartment, turned the locks, then the doorknob, and pulled the heavy steel door open. Then Fluffy was out in the hallway. She turned and looked back at the professor. Riordan thought he could see sadness in her eyes.

"I think I'll use the stairs," she said. "It's a long way down, but safer than getting caught in the elevator. Goodbye, Dad. I love you."

Fluffy opened the door to the stairwell, and then she was gone.

The sun was just going down and it was beginning to rain. It rained nearly every day now that the hundred-year drought was over. *Making up for lost time I suppose*, thought Fluffy. She found a hedge where she could hide near the path that led through the landscaped gardens in front of the building to the promenade above the harbor. Her feet hurt after that long walk down, and she needed to rest. The feel of the drizzle wetting her fur was a new sensation, and not a very pleasant one. Once it was dark, she scurried from one covert to another, around to the landward side of the building, and headed west, into the heart of the city.

Every fiber of her being, every warning sensor, was on high alert. Her heart beat madly. She tried to process the flood of new smells—plants, garbage, other animals, the wet pavement—all of it was foreign to her. The hard, wet sidewalk made her feet cold and damp.

At first, the streets were dark, lined with elegant apartment buildings and trees. It was easy to hide in the shadows, crouching under parked cars, ducking under hedges. She kept getting non-verbal pulls. She knew they were from Jack. He seemed to be guiding her in a westerly direction, away from the harbor and the posh East Side. Then, from behind her, she heard an ominous sound. A giant truck with a huge cylindrical tank on its back came whooshing up the street. It had laser eyes that swept either side of the street about a foot off the ground, and a big, robotic vacuum hose on each side that could extend up to 100 feet and follow and suck up any lone animal it sensed. Fluffy darted under a hedge and froze. When the red beam approached, she jumped straight up into the hedge and dug her claws in. The laser passed beneath her. As the truck lumbered slowly by, she read the words ANIMAL CONTROL on the side.

The second cross street she came to was dark and deserted, so she started across. But all at once a car came careening out of an alley and two headlights were bearing down on her at a frightening speed. She was right in the middle of the street. She couldn't decide whether to turn back or keep going, so she froze. Just as she was about to be run over, there was a screeching of brakes. The driver laid on his horn and Fluffy took off running. "Stupid cat!" she heard him yell. She had no idea cars could travel that fast.

After that, each time she crossed a street, she looked both ways to make sure no lights were approaching and then sprinted to the other side.

After several blocks, the houses started to look seedy and run down. Up ahead, she could see a big bright avenue with heavy traffic. As the cars stopped at the light, the ghostly whir of a hundred solar fusion turbines whispered. There was no way she would be able to get across without being seen. She retreated into someone's front yard, surrounded by a hedge, a few houses from the corner. A lone tree stood in the yard. As she sat behind the hedge and tried to think what to do, there was a horrible sound behind her. A big black dog rushed out of the doorway of the building, barking furiously, and charged straight for her. Fluffy didn't have time to think; she scrambled up the trunk of the tree and managed to gain purchase on a sturdy branch about twelve feet above the yard. The dog stayed under the tree, looking up at her and barking to raise the dead. She was certain that someone would soon come out and discover her, and her adventure would be over before it began. She inched her way out on the branch, which extended over the sidewalk and the street. Now she was at the end of the branch, as far away from the dog as possible. Cars and trucks passed below her, headed for the big avenue. When the light turned red, a line of cars stopped. There was a small truck with an open back beneath her.

In the truck bed was a tarp, which looked relatively soft. There was nothing else for her to do: she jumped off the branch and into the truck. Luckily, she landed in a spot on the tarp with nothing hard underneath it and she was not hurt. She quickly crawled under the tarp. There were cardboard cartons under there in various sizes and a metal thing with wheels and a handle. In a moment she felt the truck start up again.

After the superstorms and tidal waves of the late twenty-first century, New York City had to be abandoned, and Kingston had become the new New York. Fluffy's truck traversed busy avenues. The noise and lights of the city were frightening. Fluffy poked her head up and watched the city fly by. She didn't know where she was going but trusted that somehow Jack would guide her to him.

The truck stopped at a light near the heart of the city. Fluffy popped her head up. Lights were blazing; there was music and electricity in the air. There were theaters, nightclubs, and bars. A group of young kids—teenagers, Fluffy thought—gathered on the corner. Then there came the sound of very loud music, with a heavy, thumping rhythm. The ear-splitting noise was coming from a lone boy who approached the group, riding on an airboard. "Wow, Joey," said a girl, "you got a Miniblaster!"

"Yep," said Joey, hopping off the board and stylishly flipping it vertical with his foot. He brandished a tiny silver disc that hung around his neck on a chain. All the kids started dancing to the horrible noise. The light changed and Fluffy moved on.

After a while, the truck entered a deserted industrial neighborhood on the west side of town. Fluffy saw gangs of young men smashing car windows with big sticks.

The truck drove down dark dismal streets, slowed down, pulled into a parking lot, and stopped. A large garage door slowly rolled open. The truck drove inside the warehouse. The door lowered and the lights inside came on. Fluffy peered out from under the tarp. It was a large industrial space. The building looked and smelled old. At the far end was a loft with a metal staircase leading up to it. On it was a desk, a computer, some chairs, and a long wooden workbench against the far wall. Over the workbench were some old-fashioned frosted glass windows divided into small square panes that let in some light from the city outside. One thing that didn't seem old: there was a big flat screen on the left wall.

Two men got out of the truck. The first man was a tall black man in his twenties with a perfectly-shaped head, shaved smooth as a cue ball. The other man was white, shorter, about thirty-five. He wore a knit cap and an olive drab military-style jacket, and had a long scar down the side of his face. He looked scary. Fluffy's heart was beating so hard she was sure the men must hear it. But they calmly proceeded to pull back the tarp and shove it carelessly aside, and Fluffy stayed under it. She was now crouched in the corner of the truck bed, covered by the rumpled tarp. "Grab the dolly, Rudy," said the scary white man. Rudy lifted the metal contraption out of the truck bed and extended the handle. Each man grabbed a box, and they started stacking them on the dolly. As soon as both men had their backs turned, Fluffy made her move. She leaped out of the other side of the truck, streaked to the nearest wall, and hid behind some lumber that was leaning against it.

The men finished unloading the boxes, which they stacked neatly under the loft. There were stacks of many similar boxes already there. Most of the boxes said EPSILON on them. Fluffy recognized the name. It was the biggest robotics company and hence the most successful corporation in the world—part of the Triumvirate. The men got back in the truck, opened the garage door, and left, plunging the warehouse into darkness.

Fluffy felt safe for the first time since she had left the apartment. Her eyes quickly adjusted to the darkness. She trotted around the place, sniffing all the boxes and crates, and investigating every corner. She smelled the presence of what she thought were other animals. When she went up the stairs to the loft, the scent got stronger. Under the workbench was a row of wooden crates. Each one had a soft, fairly clean blanket neatly folded in the bottom. She hopped into one. It was extremely comfortable. Another creature had definitely occupied this space.

Then came a small voice: "Who's been sleeping in *my* bed?" it said in a mock-scary voice, then, in a light and friendly tone, "Hi! You GAB?" It was a funny, high-pitched-yet-masculine voice with a heavy New

York accent, and it was inside her head. *There's no sound. He's speaking telepathically!* Unlike the visceral feelings of distress she was getting from Jack, these were actual words.

"Yes. Yes, I am!" said Fluffy. "Where are you?"

"Come out from under the workbench and look above you."

Cautiously, Fluffy came out and looked up. There on the workbench, gazing down at her, was a little gray creature with black button eyes.

"*What* are you?" said Fluffy.

"A mouse, silly. Haven't you ever seen a mouse before?"

"I've seen pictures, but never the real thing. You don't look at all like Mickey Mouse."

"You should see me in white gloves. You got a name, kitty?"

"Fluffy. What's yours?"

"They call me Hacker."

"Are we communicating telepathically?"

"Of course. You act surprised. You've never spoken telepathically before?"

"Never without a computer giving me a voice."

"So you haven't been around other GABs, huh?"

"In all my life, I've only talked to my dad—er—my human. The professor."

"Oh, an ivory tower princess, eh? Welcome to the world, Princess."

Unused to sarcasm, Fluffy was a trifle annoyed. "It's Fluffy."

"Right. What brings you here, Fluffy?"

"I left home to look for my lost brother, and I jumped into that truck... Where am I anyhow?"

"It's a secret."

"Well, my brother is near here somewhere. I can feel him."

"Is that a fact?"

"Yes. And I've decided to join the GAB resistance. Would you happen to know anything about that?"

"Maybe I would and maybe I wouldn't. Why do you wanna join?"

"Because I can no longer sit idly by while my fellow GABs are being slaughtered."

"Good answer. What if I told you I could get you into the resistance?"

"What would I have to do?"

"Swear an oath of loyalty and obedience."

He kind of sounds like John Garfield in The Postman Always Rings Twice, *thought Fluffy. I wonder why I feel like just jumping up there and eating him.*

"I heard that," said Hacker. "You wanna eat me 'cause that's your instinct. Just like my instinct is telling me to run like hell. But we're not gonna give in to our instincts, are we, Fluffy? We can't, not if we're gonna unite and fight the humans."

"You mean, *you…*"

"Yeah, me—and some others. But you have to swear you'll never give us away and you'll sacrifice your life if need be to save our kind."

"I swear. But I don't want to hurt anyone. I want to save the GABs, but I'm not sure violence is the answer," said Fluffy.

"Oh yeah? What do you think the answer is?"

"My dad said we've got to hone our skills of telepathy and telekinesis—skills the humans don't have. Make them need us."

"Need us for what?"

"I'm not sure yet."

And that's when she got the first flash. Suddenly, in her brain, she saw a sign, just like an online popup. It had graphics: an illustration of a grand manor house in a grove of trees. The text read:

HONE YOUR SKILLS. DOG SKILLS. CAT SKILLS… ANIMAL U

"Wow, what was that?" said Fluffy

"What was what?" said Hacker.

"You didn't see it? I just had a vision. Something about 'Animal U.'"

"Animal U, huh? What else did it say?"

"Let me try to show it to you." Fluffy conjured up the vision in her mind and tried to send it to Hacker.

"Yeah, I see it! 'Hone your skills, dog skills, cat skills'… ha-ha, 'cat skills!' I get it, like the Catskill Mountains, right up there." Hacker pointed his tail in a westerly direction.

"Of course; it was a clue," said Fluffy. "That's where Animal U is, in the mountains. I wonder what they do up there."

"Homework I bet." It was another voice, a youthful tenor. A white-and-orange short-haired cat had appeared beside Hacker. "Hi, I'm Tigger," he said.

At this, Hacker, in a somewhat louder voice, in the telepathic equivalent of yelling over his shoulder, called, "She's okay, girls, you can come out now." And, as if by magic, two more beings appeared beside Hacker and Tigger on the workbench: A white mouse and a shaggy, buff-colored dog. "Fluffy, this is my posse: Tigger, Mitzi, and Fang. Posse, this is Fluffy. She wants to join up."

"How do you do," said Fluffy.

"How do you know she's not a D.I.S. spy?" cried Mitzi in a high, squeaky voice.

"Don't worry, honey," said Hacker. "I've got a sixth sense about these things."

"Wow," said Tigger, "you're a looker! Do you have reproductive organs?" Fluffy didn't quite know whether or not to be offended, so she answered civilly.

"I-I'm afraid I don't really know."

"There's no eating each other!" Mitzi chimed in nervously.

"I know the rules, but I am getting rather hungry—and you do look frightfully delicious," said Fluffy, doing her best Katharine Hepburn.

"Quick, show her where the food is!" squeaked Mitzi.

"I'll get it," said Fang in the world-weary voice of a young woman who's seen it all. And she telekinetically dragged a bag of kibble out from under the workbench, then a metal bowl. Fang lifted the bag and poured the food into the bowl without spilling a granule. Another metal bowl containing water appeared beside it. "Bon appetit," she said.

"Thank you very much," said Fluffy, impressed, and began to eat. She hadn't eaten in a long time. At length, she looked up at Fang. "Are you a dog?" she asked.

"Yes, yes, I'm a dog. That's what I am."

"Sorry. I'm kind of new to the world," said Fluffy.

"So I gathered," said Fang.

"With a name like Fang, I thought you were a boy dog."

"No, I'm a girl dog. A little joke my humans played when they got me."

"Oh...oh...*ironic* humor, right?"

"Yes," said Fang patiently, "ironic humor."

She kind of sounds like Ava Gardner in Mogambo, thought Fluffy, this time making sure she didn't broadcast her thought telepathically. "What's in those boxes?" she asked. "I didn't like the look of those humans. Maybe we should get out of here..."

"Relax," said Hacker. "They're with us."

"Really? You mean, all this is yours?"

"Yep, this is our hideout."

"And the boxes?"

"You'll see," said Hacker. "We'll talk about it in the morning. Our partners will be back by then, and we can discuss the plan. Let's get some sleep. There should be an extra crate for you to sleep in, Fluffy. A while back Animal Control got Sammy."

Fluffy didn't ask about Sammy. She was too tired and she already had plenty to think about. She missed her dad. She missed the smell of his armpit. She wished he would brush the fragments of hedge out of her tangled fur, but she cleaned herself off as best she could, and fell asleep.

CHAPTER TWO — THE PLAN

Fluffy was awakened early the next morning by the sound of the big garage door rolling open. A fleeting sliver of a dream lingered for an instant in her brain. She was in a beautiful forest, no sign of anything made by man. *This is how it should be*, she thought, *everything pristine, perfect*. Then she looked up and saw a wolf, and she knew it would eat her.

The cream-colored pickup drove in, containing the two men, the men she had taken for enemies. And a third person, a woman.

"Wake up, everybody," shouted Hacker from his perch on the workbench above. "The meeting will come to order." For the benefit of the humans, his voice came through the speakers on the computer.

Hacker introduced Fluffy to the three humans. The shorter white man was called Giuseppe, the tall black man was Rudy, and the slim young blond woman was Janet. They were all animal activists, ready to do anything in defense of the GABs.

"Giuseppe and Rudy are master thieves," said Hacker. "That's how we get all our supplies: food, the computer, the flatscreen, and the robopets. But I'll come to that… Right, here's the plan. Giuseppe, the map and the floor plan, please."

Giuseppe took his handheld from his pocket and projected the two documents on the big screen so all could see.

"On the left is the map," said Hacker. "The red dot shows where we're going to stop the A.C. truck. It's a very narrow stretch of Hope Street—right near here, as a matter of fact. Janet will be in the pickup with the hood raised and the emergency lights flashing. It will block the street, so the truck will have to stop..."

"Uh, excuse me. Sorry to interrupt," said Fluffy, "but could you tell me in a few words just what's going to happen, Hacker?"

"We're gonna hijack an Animal Control truck, free the animals, replace them with robot animals fitted with explosives—that's what's in those boxes—drive the A.C. truck into the Extermination Center, hack into the A.C. computer, unlock all the cells, free all the animals, and blow the whole place up," said Hacker. "Does that sum it up pretty well for ya?"

"So, when you blow the place up, you're going to kill the people?"

"The bad people, yeah," said Hacker.

"I won't do it." Fluffy was adamant. "I won't be part of any violence. Sabotage maybe, but not killing. Look, my dad the professor is a very wise man, and he told me something before I left home. He said 'humans are the most violent species on Earth. Don't try to beat them at their game.' If we start killing people, it will set off a chain reaction of events that will be very bad for our cause, and lots of us will get killed."

There was a moment of silence, then everybody began to speak at once. "They're the killers," screamed Mitzi.

"They're killing us, let's kill them back!" said Tigger.

"The people at these extermination centers are monsters. Believe me, I know," said Janet.

"Wait, wait!" said Giuseppe. "I think Fluffy has a good point. Killing people will make us look like the bad guys. We have a chance to get public opinion on our side. We could free the animals without hurting anyone—we can just put them to sleep with the Livion."

"Let's take a vote," said Fang.

"Okay," said Hacker, "we'll vote on it. All in favor of blowing up the Extermination Center, say 'aye.'"

Mitzi and Tigger said "aye."

"All opposed, say 'nay.'"

Fluffy, Fang and Giuseppe said "nay."

"Janet?"

There were tears of rage in Janet's eyes. "Blow 'em up," she said, almost in a whisper.

"What about you, Rudy? You haven't said anything."

"I don't know," said Rudy, looking over at Janet. "I guess I abstain."

There was a brief silence. Then Hacker said, "So it's up to me." Hacker paced back and forth on the workbench, mulling it over.

"Giuseppe, your point about PR is a good one. I say we hold off on the whole operation for a few days. I gotta think about this some more."

"What's there to think about?" said Tigger. "Either we kill 'em or we don't."

"No," said Hacker, "it's not that simple. What's bothering me is, why is it so easy for *them* to kill *us*?"

"Because we're not human," said Fang.

"Exactly. So what is it we lack that would make the humans believe we were more like them?"

"A voice," said Fluffy.

"Yes. A voice we can take with us wherever we go. Without a computer to make our thoughts audible, we're just the same as any dumb animal to them. If only there were something very small that could emit a lot of sound…"

"You mean, like a Miniblaster?" said Fluffy.

"Yes! How do you know about Miniblasters?"

"I saw—that is, I heard one out on the street. Boy, was it loud."

"Fluffy, I think you've hit on something. Giuseppe, Rudy, do you think you could get me a few of those?"

"Sure," said Giuseppe. "Just give us until tomorrow."

"Think of it," said Hacker, "being able to speak out in our own voice, anyplace, anytime. Now that would be a real revolution."

The Miniblaster was made by the electronics giant, WorldAsia, part of the Triumvirate. That night, the WorldAsia warehouse was broken into and two thousand Miniblasters were stolen.

While Rudy, Janet, and Giuseppe were out pulling the heist, Hacker and Mitzi stayed behind and worked into the night, perfecting the other component of the invention, a microprocessor that could be installed in the guts of the Miniblaster that mimicked the computer program that made thoughts into audible words.

Near dawn, the band of burglars returned with the Miniblasters and Hacker assembled the first prototype. The posse had raided a Petco weeks earlier to get food and had acquired a few cases of pet collars in various sizes, but there were none small enough for a mouse, so Janet donated a small bracelet, which Rudy made even smaller until it fit around Hacker's neck. Everyone waited in breathless anticipation as he activated the prototype. Hacker thought for a moment. Then his words rang out, loud and clear: "Creatures of the world, unite!" Everyone let out a loud cheer, but the computer had been turned off, so all the humans heard was a bark, a squeak, and two meows.

Then they all worked together to assemble a voice disc (that's what they decided to call them) for each four-legged member of the posse. Each found a collar in the cache of stolen collars and put their voice disc around their neck. Rudy made Mitzi a collar from the rest of Janet's bracelet. Then, each, in turn, tested his or her voice. They all worked beautifully, and they were thrilled with their new, audible voices.

"I've decided to cast my vote in favor of nonviolence," said Hacker. There were grumbles from the dissenters, but the die was cast. "We sleep today, and tonight—Operation Liberatis!"

"What do we do with all the animals we liberate?" asked Fluffy.

Silence.

"Uh oh, here we go again," said Tigger.

And then Fluffy got her second flash. The same illustration, the Animal U logo, but this time the inscription read: GIVE ME YOUR TIRED, YOUR POOR, YOUR HUDDLED MASSES YEARNING TO

BREATHE FREE… I LIFT MY LAMP BESIDE WEST KILL FALLS.

"Did you see that?" cried Fluffy. "Did you see that?"

"See what?"

Everyone mumbled at once. It was clear Fluffy was the only one who was getting these flashes.

"Look, I'll show it to you." And Fluffy recreated her vision and sent it out to everyone. There were murmurs of puzzlement.

"Where is West Kill Falls?" asked Fluffy.

"It's on West Kill Mountain," said Giuseppe. He took out his handheld and projected a map of the Catskills. An arrow on the screen zeroed in on the spot. "Here it is, one of the highest peaks in the Catskills, about thirty miles northwest of here on Route 28."

"That's where Animal U is, I'm sure of it," said Fluffy.

"What's Animal U?" asked everyone at once.

"I think Animal U is a secret university for GAB animals to hone their special skills," said Fluffy. "Maybe we're supposed to take all these liberated animals up there."

"Are you kidding?" said Hacker. "We're talking about, like, 100 animals here!"

"Yes," said Fluffy. "It's a problem."

"Well, isn't it enough to set them free? Do we have to take them with us? Why not just turn 'em loose and get the hell out of there?" said Tigger.

"They'd only get caught again and exterminated," said Fluffy. "No, we have to find a way to get them to Animal U."

"How 'bout we load them all into the A.C. trucks and drive them up there in a convoy?" suggested Rudy.

"Are you nuts?" said Hacker. "How far do you think we'd get with five stolen A.C. trucks loaded with 100 animals? About ten feet, I think."

A long silence, then:

"I think I got it," said Fang. Everyone shut up and listened. Fang didn't speak very often. She had been abused by her humans and was very circumspect, but when she did, she usually had something to say.

"We put the liberated animals—and ourselves— in the robot animal boxes and disguise us all as robopets. We load the boxes onto a big truck that looks like an Epsilon truck, have Giuseppe and Rudy, dressed as Epsilon drivers, drive the truck up the mountain, and hope to hell the cops go for it."

After a long pause, Hacker said, "Y'know, it just might work." Everyone excitedly expressed their approval.

"You know, Fang, you're pretty smart," said Fluffy. "...for a dog." And she telepathically sent her a smiley-face.

Fang looked at Fluffy. Her brown eyes shone with emotion, her tongue drooped out, and she smiled—in a way that dogs can and cats can't.

"So, this means the operation is postponed again," said Hacker. "We need to steal a big truck and disguise it as an Epsilon truck. Better yet, let's steal a real Epsilon truck. No, scratch that, they'll be looking for it. We disguise a stolen truck as an Epsilon truck and we get a couple of Epsilon uniforms for Giuseppe and Rudy."

"What about me?" asked Janet.

"You follow in the pickup," said Hacker, "we may need to use it for a quick getaway. There are plenty of other details too, like, how are we going to get all those animals packed up in the robot boxes and loaded into the truck before the A.C. people and the cops get after us?"

They didn't know how long it would take them to solve all the logistics problems, but Fluffy felt a particular sense of urgency. Every minute that passed meant more animals were being murdered.

CHAPTER THREE — THE TRIUMVIRATE

Jeremiah Epps called the senior management meeting to order. "I invited Chief Davis of the D.I.S. here to discuss the recent robot thefts," said Epps. The D.I.S. was the Department of Internal Security, the overarching law enforcement organization in the Western Hemisphere. Davis headed up the Northeastern U.S. Division.

Epps, a paunchy man in his fifties, was the fifth generation of Epps patriarchs to own Epsilon. He had thinning gray hair, doughy white skin, and the straight nose and blue eyes of the white, Anglo-Saxon patrician class of old—a rarity in today's racial mish-mash. And he wore glasses—amber-tinted glasses. Now, practically no one actually needed to wear glasses anymore. These days, any vision defect could be cured with some form of laser surgery, or in the worst cases, contact lenses. No, Jeremiah Epps wore tinted glasses to hide the fact that he had a false eye—a fully-functional ocular implant, to be precise. It enabled him to see just fine, but at the time he had the surgery, they hadn't quite perfected the cosmetics of it, so it looked a little creepy. A cat which he had been tormenting scratched out his left eye when he was a child. He had never been fond of animals, but from that day on he hated them.

Jeremiah Epps's great, great grandfather, Lucien Epps, was a visionary; the Henry Ford of renewable energy. With his revolutionary series of mega-storage batteries that could power everything from cars to homes to factories, he obliterated the fossil fuel industry practically single-handedly. His vision was not simply to get rich—he was rich—but to change the world, to reverse global warming and close the income gap. He accomplished those goals during his lifetime. But gradually, through the subsequent Epps dynasties that controlled Epsilon, the company reverted to the old, greed-based corporate credo of "bottom line, first, last, and always."

Now Epsilon was part of the Triumvirate, the consortium of the three largest corporations that ruled the world: Epsilon in the Western Hemisphere and some Pacific islands, WorldAsia in Asia and Australia, and Pharmacor in Europe and Africa. All national governments were subservient to the Triumvirate. Since so-called democratic elections had become a joke anyway, with the mega-corps buying the candidates who would do their bidding, the charade of elections was eventually done away with and the corporations simply appointed politicians to lead nations and states.

The companies owned by the Triumvirate supplied ninety-nine percent of the world's goods and services. They had replaced millions of human workers with specialized robots. At first, this resulted in mass riots and breadlines. So, to avoid social unrest, and to placate the now-unemployed masses, the Triumvirate built residential communities for all the people who did not have the high-tech or business skills needed to become executives, scientists, or politicians. They were called Recipient Communities (*ripcoms*) but were more like refugee camps. They were hastily-constructed bunker-like barracks where multiple families had to share a few rooms. The camps were surrounded by barbed wire fences and guarded by armed human and robot guards. People coming in and going out had to show their I.D. and explain the reason for their entrance or exit. The Recipients, as they were called, were given food ration coupons which enabled them to survive, but not much more. The patrician corporate class, which included all employable professionals, were called the Contributors. These terms were eventually shortened to *rips* and *cons*.

The Triumvirate also subsidized the arts and sports, human skills that could not as yet be matched by robots. So the arts flourished, as did athletic accomplishments.

The corporations still managed to be massively profitable because, although they paid out huge amounts in subsidies, they also made huge profits because robot labor was virtually free.

The world was now without wars and all countries shared the same currency and standard of living. And all countries had a few cons and many rips. Robot and human soldiers maintained the peace. The practice of religion, which was seen as the root cause of most conflicts, was banned, except in certain approved houses of worship and in the privacy of one's home. Any public demonstration of religious zeal was immediately and forcefully squelched.

But, in their wisdom, the corporations realized that to truly placate the masses and consolidate their absolute power, the masses needed someone to hate, a common enemy to rally against. History had taught them that, for humans to kill and torture without conscience, they had to believe that their victims were either not or less than human. And so, Jeremiah Epps convinced the other two oligarchs who controlled the world, Ho Chung Tanaka of WorldAsia, and Heinrich Himmelmann of Pharmacor, that accusing GAB animals of being terrorists would be a great solution. There was no question that they were not human, and their strange powers scared people. And thus began the great campaign against animal terrorism.

All of the principals of Epsilon's upper management were gathered at the long table in Meeting Room A, which was on the top floor of the two hundred-story Epsilon Building in downtown Kingston. Two walls of the room were floor-to-ceiling windows that provided a spectacular view of the Kingston harbor to the east and the mountains to the north. Present were: Ahmet Patel, CFO and VP Finance, a small brown man in his forties, Aurora Malvolio-Jones, VP Communications, a tall woman of mixed lineage in her thirties, Jorge Peña, VP Sales, a man in his fifties of Latino descent (all sales executives in all of the fifteen divisions of Epsilon reported to him, including Larissa Jacobi, VP Robot Sales, a short woman of mixed lineage, who sat beside him at the table), and Terrence Baker, VP Marketing for all 15 divisions, a tall, fair-haired man in this thirties. Seated next to Epps on his right was his second in command, Valerie Trump, Senior VP Operations. She was a sleek, dark-haired woman in her thirties, who appeared to have a mixture of Asian and European lineage. On his left was Epps's secretary, Charlotte Beauchamp, who recorded the meeting.

Epps was not pleased. He scrolled through the quarterly earnings reports one more time. One item kept jumping out at him, glaring, mocking: LOSSES DUE TO THEFT. Hundreds of robots had been stolen from Epsilon warehouses. The people who were supposed to be guarding them had been anesthetized quickly and silently. They never saw who did it. The warehouse computers were hacked so expertly, the records doctored to hide the loss, that they couldn't tell for weeks just how many robots had been stolen.

The missing robots were all from Epsilon's new line of robot pets. They were perfectly life-like dogs and cats, available in a wide assortment of breeds and sizes. They had the latest enhanced features: realistic skin and fur, moist eyes and mouths, a pulse, simulated breathing, and the newest feature: body heat. They were programmed to play, bark, meow, purr, pant, chase balls, catch Frisbees, and display affection, just like real pets. They were actually superior to real animals, in that you never had to feed them or walk them, and they never pooped, peed, or threw up. And they never scratched or bit you.

Chief Davis sat at the far end of the long table. "Well, Chief," said Epps, "what have you got for us?"

"We know it was done by some kind of animal terrorist group," said Davis.

Morgan Davis was a former beat cop who had worked his way up through the ranks. He was a huge black man in his mid-fifties; still an imposing physical specimen, though now a bit soft in the belly. "They left a sort of calling card."

"What was that?"

"It's a paw print, spray-painted with a stencil on the warehouse wall." The Chief showed everyone an enlarged photo of the symbol. It was hard to tell if it was the print of a dog or a cat.

"How did they get in?" asked Epps.

"We don't know. The robot sentinels were all deactivated and the human guards were given Livion gas. It knocked them out, and they remembered nothing. The same group used the same M.O. to hijack a bunch of pet food from a Petco a couple of weeks ago, and just the other night, they stole some Miniblasters from a WorldAsia warehouse."

"Hmm, now why would they do that? Maybe all these thefts are tied into some kind of master plan… Are you going to introduce us to your associate?" asked Epps, indicating a pale, thin man sitting in a chair, not at the table, in the corner.

"Oh, sorry. That's Zvonar," said the chief. "He's a new Special Investigator in the Animal Terrorism unit."

Zvonar gave Epps a cursory nod, his face expressionless.

"What are his qualifications?" asked Epps, somewhat annoyed. He was used to being consulted about new hires in the Animal Terrorism unit.

"He has no law enforcement credentials," said Davis. "His only qualification is that he is psychic."

"Psychic?"

"Yes, he can pick up the telepathic communications between the GABs. A very valuable qualification, wouldn't you agree?"

"Yes. Yes, I would agree. Got any leads yet, Mr. Zvonar?"

"I hear many voices," said Zvonar in a vaguely European accent. "The hard part is figuring out who is saying what to whom. Proximity is a factor. Get me close enough to the terrorists, and I will hear their plans."

"Well, if we knew where they were, we wouldn't need you, would we?" snorted Epps contemptuously. He turned back to Davis. "So you've got nothing."

"We'll get them," said Davis. "We just need more time."

"Time is money, Davis," said Epps. "Get them soon." Davis and Zvonar left the room.

Then Valerie Trump spoke up. "Frankly, Jerry, I feel we're focusing too much on robopets and petty theft, and not enough on the fact that our numbers are down across the board—in practically every division."

"I know," said Epps, annoyed. "Don't you think I know that? It's just a normal correction in the market. We were doing great for a long while, and now things have leveled off. Population shrinkage and all that."

"I don't agree," said Valerie.

"Okay, Valerie, tell us your theory."

"It's not a theory, Jerry, it's fact. Our assembly line robots are screwing up. They are making ever shoddier products, and the public is wise to it. I'm sure none of us can forget the massive recall of a million Epsilon Cruisers last July, due to one robot failing to do the one job it was programmed for, to tighten the bolts on the engine mount. Twenty-five people died, we paid out 200 million in compensation and had to recall all those cars. And then sales on that model plummeted—due to lack of faith by the public."

"So what solution do you propose?" asked Epps

"Hire more humans. Robot intelligence is not nuanced enough to conduct proper quality control of products—and that goes for cars, batteries, solar panels, vacuum cleaners, breakfast cereals—everything. Put well-trained humans in charge of quality control everywhere. Plus, it will take more people off the welfare rolls and out of the ripcoms."

"I disagree. That car recall was an anomaly. For my money—and it is my money we're talking about here—robots are more efficient, less expensive, and superior in every way to human workers."

The growing rift between Epps and his second in command was becoming more and more evident at each meeting, both public and private.

"Can you please see me in my office?" Epps told Valerie, sotto voce, as they exited the meeting room.

"Now?"

"Now," said Epps.

Once in his office, Epps let his fury fly. "How many times have I told you, Valerie? We need to present a united front. If you have an issue with me, take it up with me here, in private, not in front of the entire staff!"

"Every time I've done that, Jerry, my 'issue' was never heard by the rest of the company. You simply squelch every idea I have. I did this today so that at least some other people get to chew on my idea other than you. Let me tell you something: you need to focus less on your pet hatreds—pun intended—and more on the legitimate concerns of running a business."

"Get out!" said Epps. "I'll let you know Monday if you still have a job."

That evening Epps was preoccupied as he ascended to the roof of the Epsilon building and climbed into his robocopter. Valerie's comments were infuriating. He was now convinced he needed to get rid of her. But his mind kept going back to his obsession: the GABs. As he flew home, he wondered what they were planning. Maybe they took the robopets just to send a message that real animals were better than robot animals. *Not true*, thought Epps. His robot pets were superior to organic animals in every way, just as the robot workers in his factories were better than the human ones ever were, regardless of what Valerie thought. He firmly believed this. He had to.

As his copter set itself down on the helipad atop his sprawling mansion, Epps's son, Lucien, a handsome young man of twenty, was just climbing into his robocopter. After getting kicked out of several fine universities, Lucien was now learning about the working world at a job his father had obtained for him at the A.C. extermination center.

"They put me on the night shift again, Dad," Lucien said. "Can't you make them give me the day shift from now on? It's so depressing at the center at night. All those pathetic animals crying and whimpering..."

"It'll toughen you up," said Epps. "I had them put you on the night shift. You need to learn the meaning of hard, distasteful work like I did."

Lucien, dressed in his navy blue Animal Control cap and coveralls, gave his father a baleful look, climbed into his robocopter, and flew off toward town.

Epps had lived in this, the family estate, all his life. The first Lucien Epps had commissioned the famous twenty-first-century architect Jared Fuller to build him an art deco dream house where Frank Lloyd Wright himself might have lived. It was a panoramic multi-level white marble ocean liner of a house; long, low and wide. He and Barbara, the mother of his two children, had lived here in relative contentment and raised their daughter and their son until two years ago. That's when Epps met Lorna.

It was at a company retreat in the Florida Islands. She was twenty-six, a year older than his daughter, beautiful, fiery, artistic. She had been hired by Epsilon to coordinate the entertainment at the retreat, and lived on Miami, the big island, in a little beach shack outside of town. Epps had fallen hard for her, and she let him. He bought Barbara a beautiful home and moved her out of his marble palace, and moved Lorna in. That's when his daughter, Janet, had left home. She joined an animal resistance group and he had heard nothing since. He didn't know where she was.

Lorna lived there with Epps for exactly one year. That's all she could take of his controlling personality and the inexorable boredom and isolation of living so far from town, alone in that giant mausoleum. Then, one day about a year ago, she was gone. Epps was devastated. She had been his reason for living, and now life was just a bad taste in his mouth. Like his daughter, Lorna had disappeared without a trace. There was no communication. She made no attempt to get money from him. Nothing.

Epps descended into his study and poured himself a tall euphorium vodka on the rocks.

CHAPTER FOUR — THE CAPER

At one-fifteen a.m. Janet sits in the pickup, staring into the rearview mirror. She's parked in the narrowest stretch of Hope Street, a dark, deserted street, a block from the hideout. There are cars parked on either side, making passing impossible. As planned, the hood is raised, and the emergency lights are flashing. At one-eighteen a.m. she sees the lights and ominous silhouette of the A.C. truck approaching. It pulls up behind her and stops. She can see there are two men in the driver's seat. The two men exchange some words, then, seeing an attractive young woman in distress, they both open their doors and get out. As soon as they do, Giuseppe and Rudy pop out from behind parked cars on both sides of the truck. They each hold an aerosol can, containing Livion. Not only does the gas render its victims unconscious for at least twelve hours, but upon waking, the victim has no memory more recent than the previous day. Giuseppe and Rudy spray the gas in the faces of the two drivers and they immediately collapse. They quickly remove the drivers' navy blue coveralls and caps and don the uniforms. Then they open the rear hatch of the cylindrical tank on the back. About twenty-five animals, half of them GAB dogs and cats, huddle inside the hold.

Fluffy, Fang, and Tigger emerge from the pickup truck and telepathically reassure the terrified GAB animals inside that they are safe. The animals leap out of the A.C. truck. About six non-GAB dogs and seven cats run off into the night. The rest—twelve GABs—are led to the pickup, where Janet is unloading twenty-five robopets and activating them. The robopets are loaded into the hold of the A.C. truck, along with the two unconscious drivers. The freed animals hop into the back of the pickup, and Janet heads for the hideout, texting Hacker that step one has been accomplished and she is on her way. The humans are all talking to each other and Hacker with text on their handhelds—the safest, least traceable way to communicate.

At the hideout, Hacker and Mitzi are on the computer, hacking into the A.C. system. Janet's text pops up in the lower right corner of the screen. Hacker knows they have just a few minutes to complete disabling the A.C. systems, but they can't do it too soon so that the people at A.C. can't raise the alarm before Rudy and Giuseppe get there.

Rudy, Giuseppe, Fluffy, Tigger, and Fang are in the cab of the A.C. truck, en route to the extermination center. At one thirty-five a.m., they reach the guard post at the outer gate. Rudy texts Hacker to disable the external cameras.

Inside the A.C. control room, young Lucien Epps mans the main console. Suddenly the monitor screens showing the areas outside the building go dark. "Hey Mike," Lucien shouts to his colleague, "the monitors have gone off."

"Oh yeah," says Mike lackadaisically, "that happens from time to time. Lemme take a look." He starts fiddling with the wiring that connects the monitors to the console.

The truck pulls up to the guard post. Giuseppe, in the driver's seat, rolls down the window, his hat pulled low over his eyes. Before the guard can say anything, he sprays him in the face, and he passes out. Rudy jumps out of the passenger side, enters the guard house, opens the gate and sits the unconscious guard up in his seat, making him look as if he's asleep.

The truck rolls to the receiving dock. Rudy and Giuseppe back the truck up to the intake chute, but before they connect the chute to the truck's rear hatch, they unload the two unconscious guards. With the help of telekinesis from Fluffy, Tigger, and Fang, they lift the guards into two empty A.C. trucks that are parked nearby. They sit the unconscious guards in the driver's seats of the two trucks. Then, Rudy, Giuseppe, Fluffy, Tigger, and Fang all get into the hold of the truck with all the robopets. Rudy texts Hacker: "Step 2 accomplished. Command intake robots to attach intake tube." The intake tube, a long, retractable tunnel, made out of ribbed plastic, like a really big vacuum cleaner hose, attaches itself to the hatch on the back of the A.C. truck. Then, Rudy, Giuseppe, Fluffy, Fang, and Tigger herd the robopets ahead of them through the intake tube. The two men and the three animals follow and enter the intake chute inside the extermination center. Oblivious to the intruders, the intake robots do the job they were programmed for: they herd the robopets, as well as Fluffy, Fang, and Tigger, into the cages, separating dogs and cats. Rudy and Giuseppe hang back, pressing themselves flat against the wall to avoid detection by the robots. Rudy texts Hacker: "Step 3 accomplished. We're in. Open cages."

Lucien Epps shouts to his partner, Mike, "We have a malfunction. The cages are unlocked!" He tries various measures to restore the power to the disabled functions, to no avail. Suddenly Rudy and Giuseppe are in the control room. They each spray one of the A.C. guys with Livion. Both Lucien and Mike pass out. Rudy finds the code to unlock the extermination chamber, unlocks it. Giuseppe opens the door that leads to the parking lot and props it open.

Fluffy approaches the extermination chamber with a strong feeling of excitement and anticipation. She turns the big wheel that seals it airtight and opens the heavy door. Inside are another twenty or thirty animals awaiting execution. At first, they just stand there, frozen with fear. "It's okay," says Fluffy, "you're free now. Follow the other animals to the trucks." The doomed animals are huddled together in a corner of the room, quivering. Fluffy turns on her voice disc. "Come on, you're safe. Walk out the door and straight ahead. I'll be right behind you." Their ears prick up at hearing an audible voice from a GAB. Then, very slowly, almost reluctantly, they file out of the chamber. Fluffy waits until they are all out. But there is one skinny gray and white cat that doesn't move.

"Fluffy?"

"Jack!"

"I knew you would find me." They rub up against each other joyously.

"Come on," says Fluffy, "there's no time." And Jack, looking frail and wobbly, follows Fluffy down the corridor.

Fluffy, Fang, and Tigger tell all the freed GAB animals to quickly and calmly make their way to the intake chute, to go through the hose and get in the hold of the A.C. truck parked outside. Jack follows. The robopets stay in the cages. The non-GABs—about fifty of them—run out the open door to the parking lot and scatter in all directions.

Rudy whips out the stencil and a can of black spray paint and sprays the posse's logo on the wall. Then he texts Hacker: "Step 4 accomplished. Loading animals now." When the hold of the first truck is full, Giuseppe starts it up and drives it a few feet toward the main gate. Rudy climbs into the cab of one of several parked A.C. trucks not in use and starts it up. He pulls it up behind the first truck and opens the hatch. They load up the second truck and it pulls forward. Now Fluffy climbs into one of the A.C. trucks containing an unconscious driver, and Fang climbs into the other. Although the trucks are self-driving, they are programmed not to function unless someone weighing at least 100 lbs. is in the driver's seat, hence the unconscious drivers. Fluffy and Fang program their trucks to pull up behind the others and they, in turn, are loaded with liberated animals.

All four trucks are loaded to capacity, but there are still about a dozen animals left in the intake chute. Tigger stays with them, reassuring them that they too will be taken out. As the four big A.C. trucks pull out, heading for the hideout, Janet pulls up in the pickup. "C'mon!" she yells, and Tigger leads the remaining animals, including Jack, into the back of the pickup. Jack is too weak to make the jump; Tigger gives him a telekinetic boost.

Janet texts Rudy: "Is everybody out?"

"Yes."

"Are you sure?"

"Yes."

In her hand, Janet holds a small cylinder the size of a roll of quarters with a button on top. She follows the A.C. trucks out the main gate. When they are about 200 feet up the street, she pushes the button on the detonator.

CHAPTER FIVE — THE SIEGE

"I just had to do it." Janet stands rigid, her face frozen into a mask of cold remorse. Only her glistening eyes betray her emotion. "I've hated that place ever since I was a little girl. They've been slaughtering innocent animals there for twenty years. I just wanted to see it obliterated from the face of the Earth."

The entire posse and their over 100 guests are assembled in the vast warehouse hideout which now, crowded with animals and two trucks, does not seem so vast.

They've pulled the pickup truck inside, as well as the big truck they were going to disguise as an Epsilon truck and use for their getaway.

"Janet, do you realize what you've done?" says Hacker. "You've put the kibosh on the whole operation. What are we supposed to do now? The cops and A.C. will be everywhere looking for us. And what are we supposed to do with those four A.C. trucks? They're like having a neon sign in our front yard!"

"And you killed people, Janet. Two of them." says Fluffy. "We said we weren't going to kill anyone!"

"I'm sorry, but I hate Animal Control and everyone that works for them. As for the trucks, I'll drive one of them. We can program the other three to follow. The two drivers are still out cold and sitting in the driver's seats. We just need to put 100 lbs. of weight in the fourth one. If they catch me, they catch me."

"You can't get caught," says Hacker. "They'll torture you until you lead them to us. But we do need to get those trucks out of here now. Where can we take them before it gets light?"

"There's a Sanitation Department parking lot, not five blocks from here," says Giuseppe. "Maybe we can park them among the garbage trucks. It might buy some time before they find them. If we wipe them clean and hope we didn't leave any DNA, finding the trucks won't help them find us, as long as we stay here."

"We have to act fast," says Rudy. "Giuseppe and I will go with you, Janet, and we'll take the pickup so we can get back." Janet, Giuseppe, and Rudy head out to the parking lot.

Fluffy regards her brother. "Jack, you look terrible. So thin and weak."

"You'd be thin and weak too if you'd been living out of garbage cans your whole life, and then kept a prisoner in that place."

"I'm so sorry. I wish I had gone to look for you sooner. I've been hearing your voice in my head for years." Then she announces, "Everyone, this is my brother, Jack."

Hacker, Mitzi, Fang, and Tigger all introduce themselves to Jack and make sure he gets extra food.

Racing against the dawn, the convoy sets out, staying on the backstreets. They can hear the sounds of sirens and helicopters everywhere. They drive without headlights, park the trucks in the Sanitation lot, which is not locked or guarded, wipe the trucks clean of prints, leave the two drivers asleep at the wheel, and drive back to the hideout quickly. Hacker opens the door and the pickup rolls in.

"So, I guess this means no trip to the mountains," says Fang dryly.

"We're not going anywhere," says Hacker. "All we can do now is hunker down here and hope this thing blows over in a few days—or weeks. Unless they find us…"

"Don't even say that!" squeals Mitzi.

"You mice'll be okay," says Fang. "You can literally fade into the woodwork. But the rest of us…"

On the big screen, the news is coming on. There are aerial shots of the still-flaming rubble of the extermination center.

"The remains of two bodies have been found in the wreckage. Police say it will be several days before their identities can be confirmed, but they are believed to be the two guards on duty inside the facility: Michael Burns and Lucien Epps III, twenty-year-old son of Epsilon president Jeremiah Epps…"

"Noooo!" shrieks Janet, and she collapses to the floor, sobbing uncontrollably. The posse gathers around her. All the liberated animals listen in silence.

"What is it, Janet?" says Hacker.

"I killed my brother!" she wails. "Lucien Epps was my kid brother!"

"Then you're the daughter of…"

Janet looks up at them. "That's right. I'm the daughter of that bastard, Jeremiah Epps."

The room falls under a long, oppressive silence. At length, Hacker speaks: "Prepare for a siege!"

They back the two trucks up against the front door; they hang blackout curtains over the row of windows at the back. Earlier, they had made giant litter boxes out of lumber and sand. For the animals that knew how to use them, the toilets were fitted with animal potty seats—toilet seats with a smaller hole and a flat area where an animal can sit. They had also made feeding troughs, one for dogs, one for cats, and figured out that there would be enough food for ten days only, as long as no one ate more than one meal a day. Blankets and carpeting were laid out for the guests to sleep on.

For the first day, the guests are well behaved, mostly because they're scared. But, after that, the natives get restless. A couple of playful young dogs decide to chase cats, two dogs have a noisy dispute over a sleeping spot, two male cats mark the same territory, then get into a squalling match, there are complaints about someone eating more than their share. Fluffy and the others do their best to break up the fights and maintain peace, but for a while, pandemonium reigns.

"You can't make any noise!" says Hacker, yelling in a whisper. "The enemy can hear everything!" But they pay him no mind.

Then, a venerable old Saint Bernard named Bernard steps forward and tries to get the attention of his fellow guests. Throat-clearing doesn't work, so he fixes his gaze on the two trucks that block the entrance, raises them up in the air about three feet, and lets them drop. The ground shakes with the thud. Everyone shuts up, looks back and forth between the trucks and Bernard in silent amazement. Then, in a deep commanding voice, Bernard speaks. "Listen, brothers and sisters, we are guests in this place and under the protection of these brave animals and humans who risked their lives to save us. We have to learn to overcome our base instincts and use the superior brains we're blessed with. Now, there will be no more foolishness!" After that, things get quiet.

Twelve hours pass. Janet lies in the fetal position on her mat. She neither eats, nor sleeps, nor speaks—until the second day.

"I want to give myself up," she says in a loud, shaky voice. "My father won't let them torture me, and I won't give you up. I'll die first."

"No," says Rudy. "They have drugs that can make you talk, and you won't even remember saying anything." Rudy has more than a little compassion for Janet; everyone knew there was chemistry going on between them, although it was never spoken of.

"He's right," says Hacker. "You have to stay here."

"We know you're sorry, Janet," says Fluffy. "If it makes you feel better, know that we forgive you... don't we, everyone?"

Everyone murmurs their assent. "Yes... yes, Janet, we forgive you..."

Janet musters a little smile and touches Fluffy's head.

Outside the air is buzzing with police helicopters and air cruisers. Every road out of town has a checkpoint, which causes huge traffic jams that back up for miles into the heart of the city. All private air traffic is grounded.

Chief Davis himself rushes to the scene when the A.C. trucks and the two drivers are discovered in the Sanitation lot. The drivers have just regained consciousness and, of course, remember nothing. Zvonar sits beside Davis in his robocopter.

"Tell them to touch nothing," says Zvonar. "Tell the drivers to stay exactly where they are and not move. The terrorists may have left some psychic 'scent' I can follow."

When Davis' copter touches down, Zvonar moves close to one of the trucks, stands motionless for a moment, then to the other. He climbs into the cab and sits next to the driver, who, per instructions, remains motionless in the driver's seat. The two men sit in silence for several minutes. Then, Zvonar gets down and returns to Chief Davis in the copter.

"Well?"

"They are very near here. Circle the neighborhood. They are in one of these warehouses." Zvonar gestures vaguely in a semicircle.

They fly in ever-widening circles over the neighborhood. Below are countless warehouses and industrial spaces, some abandoned. Eyes closed, Zvonar directs Davis' copter, first this way and then that. At last, they are over the hideout.

"It's that one... right down there. I can hear them!" cries Zvonar.

Davis contacts headquarters and, within ten minutes, the parking lot outside the hideout is filled with police vehicles. Davis and Zvonar are already on the scene.

Jeremiah Epps, the grieving father, also arrives, wanting to personally take charge of the annihilation of the terrorists who killed his son.

The hideout is part of a mostly-deserted industrial complex that includes several other old warehouses. The buildings are in a contiguous row; the hideout is the first one on the left. They all share the vast parking lot.

Hacker has cameras mounted outside the front door, and when the police arrive, he can see the vehicles assembling outside in the parking lot.

"They've found us!" cries Hacker, looking at the monitor screen.

"There's Epps himself!"

There is a moment of panic in the hideout. Then Janet cries, "Let me go out there. Maybe they'll let you go if I give myself up."

"Fat chance," says Hacker. "Knock out the windows and make a run for it!" He enables a virus-like worm called Tapeworm on his computers, which literally eats all the data. Then, he hurls a large hard drive through the windows, and Hacker and Mitzi disappear into the wall.

Then all hell breaks loose. Without even the customary bull-horned warning from the cops, a huge truck with a steel wedge mounted on the front crashes through the front door. It's stopped by the two trucks that are parked inside but tears an enormous hole in the corrugated metal garage door. Rudy, Giuseppe, and Janet appear with grenade launchers and fire RPGs out the damaged door that destroy a couple of police cruisers. The parking lot is turned into an instant war zone.

"This way!" shouts Fluffy from the loft. All the panicked animals run up the stairs to the loft, leap onto the workbench, and start fleeing out the broken windows.

Fluffy frantically scans the crowd. "Jack! Jack, where are you?" But she can't see him anywhere.

Outside the windows, on the street side of the building, there is a strip of roof rimmed with a low brick wall. As the animals flee out the window, a huge unmanned gunship rises up over the street like a monstrous specter. It opens fire on the animals, mowing down dozens of them.

Fluffy, Tigger, and Fang, seeing no alternative, follow the others out the window and run to the right, staying close to the brick retaining wall. Hundreds of bullets whizz over their heads. The cats stay low, but a bullet hits Fang in her side and she falls. Fluffy stops and Tigger keeps going.

"Fang!" cries Fluffy. "Can you get up?"

Fang lays on her side, her breathing labored. "Keep going, sweetie," she whispers. She's bleeding badly. "Get to the mountains, find that school…" And then she is gone.

When cats cry, there are no tears. But inside, Fluffy's tears fall like rain. She looks up at the battle drone. "You killed my friend, now GO DOWN!" If looks could kill, that battle drone would be dead, and in this case they could. The huge ship spins out of control and crashes into the street below in a ball of flames.

Another gunship appears almost immediately and starts firing on Fluffy. She runs faster than she knew she could. The bullets follow her, try to cut her down but miraculously none of them hits her. At the end of the row of contiguous buildings, there's an alley about fifteen feet wide. On the other side is another industrial building the same height. It has an air vent that looks like a curved smokestack on the roof. Without thinking, and not really caring if she falls to her death, Fluffy leaps without slowing down, without looking down. She sails over the alley and her front paws are just able to grab the edge of the other roof. She runs to the air vent and dives in, just as it is demolished by a hail of bullets. She spirals down and down, through what seems like an endless aluminum vortex, and lands with a clang. She's inside an air duct which runs horizontally beneath the ceiling of the warehouse. She stops, catches her breath, and huddles there, shaking. She thinks of her dead friend. She thinks of all her friends, and her brother, whom she will probably never see again.

It's pitch dark inside the air duct, but her cat's eyes can see a faint light in the distance, straight ahead. She knows it's probably a way out, but she just huddles there, unwilling to move. Then the earth shakes and there's a horrendous roar. Fluffy knows the hideout is no more. She wonders if any of her friends have survived.

CHAPTER SIX — LOOSE LIPS

Professor James Riordan was despondent. It had been a long while since he had gone out of the house, but with Fluffy gone he had been drinking alone and talking to himself, so he forced himself to take a shower and go to his old favorite watering hole. He entered Scully's and sat on his once-customary stool.

"Professor! Where you been? You're looking well," said Tom Scully, the bartender and owner.

"Don't bullshit me, Tom. I look like hell and I know it," said Riordan. "Glenfiddich. A double."

Scully's was a few blocks from Riordan's building. It was also one of the few remaining bars that actually served alcoholic drinks, which was probably why there were so few customers. Alcohol had gradually gone out of style with the younger generation and had been supplanted by euphorium-based drinks, a compound that was generally considered to give the ultimate euphoric high, without the discomfort of a hangover. But James Riordan had come from a long line of Irish drinking writers. He was old school.

The bar was dark and cozy, all polished mahogany and brick. Scully poured him the drink. Riordan downed it and asked for another.

"So, where ya been keepin' yourself?" asked Scully, as he poured round two.

"Nowhere. I just stay home. Day after day, night after night."

"Ahh, that's not healthy," said Scully. "Everybody needs to get out once in awhile"

"Hence, here I am," said Riordan.

Just then, a thin, scruffy guy about thirty with sandy hair and beard noticed Riordan and moved down the bar to sit beside him. "Hey, Professor Riordan, right?"

"Ex-professor."

"I was in your English Lit class—god, it must be six, eight years ago. Arthur Yellin. Do you remember me?"

Riordan turned and scrutinized the guy for a moment. "Nope, can't say I do."

"Well, I guess I wasn't much of a scholar. I dropped out after two semesters."

"So now what're you doing?" asked Riordan, trying to seem interested.

"Art. See all these paintings?" He made a sweeping gesture, indicating five large paintings that hung on the brick wall behind them. Riordan hadn't noticed the new art, but now he swiveled around gave it a long, hard look.

At length, Riordan said, "These are good. Damn good." He was not a man who doled out compliments easily. "What did you say your name was?"

"Art. Art Yellin."

"Well, Art, your art is certainly yellin' at me," quipped Riordan. He smiled his still-charming Irish smile.

"Ha-ha, good one!" said Art.

"Have you sold many?"

"Uh, not really. Wanna buy one?"

"Maybe...maybe..."

"Can I buy you a drink, professor?"

"Why don't you let me buy you one? Can't be much money in painting."

"True, but I get the government subsidy, y' know. But okay, thanks. Another of the same, Tommy."

Scully set up a brandy and soda for Art, and the two men raised their glasses. "To good old alcohol and hangovers!" said Riordan. They clinked glasses and bottoms up.

The professor got up and, weaving slightly, walked the length of the room, surveying the paintings. They were abstract, but there were recognizable objects. You could make out bits of buildings, people, and creatures. They used bold, vibrant colors, and were painted with painstaking precision—a quality Riordan admired. They drew you in. Riordan sat back down next to Art. He took a photo out of his inside jacket pocket.

"Do you think you could make a painting inspired by *her*?" he asked. It was a picture of Fluffy.

"What's this?" asked Art.

"It's my cat, Fluffy. She's gone away." And Riordan started to tear up.

"Pretty. What do you mean 'gone away'? Did she get out and wander off and get lost?"

"No. She said she wanted to find her brother and join the animal resistance movement, and I let her go." He started to choke up again. "I really miss her. Do you think you could make a painting? Not realistic; in your style. Abstract, but *inspired* by Fluffy? I'd be willing to pay—well."

"I dunno. Maybe I could," said Art tentatively.

"You can do it, Art—frame her 'fearful symmetry.'"

Art chuckled. "I seem to remember something about that in your class. Can I keep this?"

"Yeah. Here's my number. Think about it and give me a call." He wrote his number on the back of the photo.

Art fished a battered business card out of his shirt pocket and gave it to Riordan.

It said, ART BY ART and gave his number.

On the small screen mounted above the bar, the news came on. It showed the smoldering remains of the extermination center and the artillery barrage in the parking lot, ending with the cops blowing up the animal hideout. Riordan watched it with a terrible feeling of dread.

"I gotta go. Great meeting you. Bye," said Riordan, and he abruptly wheeled about and walked out of the bar and onto the dark street. He didn't notice the nondescript bald man who had been sitting alone at one of the dark tables in back and who now got up and followed him.

Riordan had just reached his building when his phone rang. "Hello?"

"Professor, it's Art." His voice was stressed.

"Hi, Art. Anything wrong?"

"Yes. I think you were followed."

Riordan keyed in his code and opened the door of his building. As he pulled the glass door open, he could see the reflection of the bald man standing under a streetlight about fifty feet behind him. The man was talking on his handheld.

"I think you're right," said Riordan, as he entered the lobby of his building and frantically pressed for the elevator while glancing over his shoulder.

"I think you talked a little too loudly about your cat," said Art.

"Listen, Art. I need you to do me a favor."

"Yes?"

"I'm going to leave my keycard under my doormat. It's apartment 15005, can you remember that?"

"I'm writing it down," said Art.

"The entry code is 34782. Write that down too."

"Okay."

"Call me in the morning. If I don't answer my phone, I want you to come over here. Let yourself into my apartment. It's nice, you'll like it. You can paint here. The light is good. Make all the mess you want. I want you to stay here until you hear from me. I want someone to be here in case Fluffy gets back or sends a message. If the D.I.S. shows up, you have no idea where I am, but I asked you to house-sit for me, okay?"

"Will I be in danger?"

"Maybe. Art, I know you hardly know me, but will you do this for me?"

"Yes."

"Bless you, Art. Wish me luck."

"Good luck, professor."

Riordan got to his floor, entered his apartment. He hurriedly packed a few things, grabbed a disc containing his half-finished novel, put on a long trench coat and a broad-brimmed fedora. On the way out he stopped in front of the full-length mirror by the front door. He rubbed his upper lip with his thumb like Jean-Paul Belmondo in *Breathless*. "Bogie," he muttered. On the way out, he left the keycard under the mat and left his home, maybe forever. He took the elevator down to the garage, which had an exit on the landward side of the building.

He knew that getting arrested by the D.I.S. for animal terrorist activities might mean being taken away and never heard from again. He knew other people, animal activists, who had been "disappeared." They had never been charged, tried, or convicted and their whereabouts were still unknown. *Well, I said I needed to get out more...*

As he walked quickly into the night, he wished he had remembered to wipe the cache on his browsers and get rid of Fluffy's tracking collar. But it was too late now. If they caught him, he was cooked. He wracked his besotted brain for where he could go, whom he could trust...

Fluffy waited until dark. Then she made her way toward where she had seen the light coming through in the daytime. About fifty feet on, she came to a vent in the duct and through it she could see below a deserted room with work tables and piles of shipping materials and baskets. There was a strong smell of baked goods and sugar; pleasant, but not appetizing. She could see that the vent was fastened in place with four screws. This would not be easy. With all her concentration, she focused on the first screw and she made it turn. *Now, what was it Dad used to say? "Lefty loosey, righty tighty."* She turned the screw to the left and slowly, slowly, it came loose and finally fell out to the floor below. Then she focused on the next screw, and the next. When the last screw came loose, the grate on the vent, which was about a foot square, fell into a basket of baked goods and didn't make a sound. Fluffy took a leap and landed in another basket. The muffins in it cushioned her fall perfectly. *Not so good for eating*, she thought, *but great for a soft landing*. She looked around.

She was in what appeared to be a bakery that made gift baskets. A large banner that decorated one wall read: MRS. MOFFET'S MUFFINS – GIFT BASKETS FOR ALL OCCASIONS. There were rows of big ovens along one wall, and there were long tables on which, by day, workers assembled the gift baskets, addressed them, and sent them out. Then Fluffy heard a rustling coming from inside one of the baskets. She went into stalking mode and snuck up on the basket. She was ready to pounce when she heard a familiar voice. "Fluffy?"

"Hacker?"

"Fluffy!" It was Mitzi.

"Hacker, Mitzi! How did you get here?"

"Mice can go places others can't. It smelled good in here, so we followed our noses," said Hacker. "Is everyone else dead?"

At this, Fluffy broke down. Between sobs, she told them, "Fang is... I watched her die... It was horrible... Tigger was with us... He kept running... I haven't seen him since. As far as I know, the others are all dead... even my brother."

"What are you gonna do now?" asked Hacker.

"I'm going to try to get to the mountains, to Animal U. Do you guys want to go with me?"

"We can't travel long distances on foot," said Hacker.

"And walking in the woods, we'd surely be eaten by something," said Mitzi. "They got owls, and hawks, and coyotes..."

"How about wolves? Are there wolves?" asked Fluffy.

"No wolves around here, just coyotes. Believe me, they're bad enough," said Hacker.

"I had a dream about a wolf..."

"I've got a great idea, Fluffy," said Hacker. "Why don't we all go to your house?"

"My house?"

"Yeah, the professor's place. I know how we can get there real easy."

"How?" said Fluffy warily.

"You see those gift baskets over there?"

"Uh huh."

"They're all wrapped with address cards and ready to be delivered. All we have to do is address a card to the professor, hide in the basket, and have ourselves delivered."

"That's fine for you guys," said Fluffy. "But aren't I a bit large to hide in a basket of muffins?"

"I thought about that," said Hacker. "All you have to do is hide by the front door until the delivery truck loads up in the morning and jump in when no one's looking. Then, when we get to your building, voila!"

Fluffy thought for a moment. "I'd love to go back home to the professor, I really would. But then all our efforts, all the lives of our friends, everything will have been for nothing. No, I've got to go on... But why don't you guys go to the professor's. You can let him know I'm alright and tell him I'm still trying to find Animal U. I'll help wrap you in the basket. Maybe the professor can help you get back in the fight. And guys..."

"Yes?"

"Tell him I love him, and I'll never forget what he taught me."

"Okay."

Hacker got on Mrs. Moffet's computer and quickly accessed the program that printed out the gift cards that were fastened to the baskets. Fluffy gave him the professor's address, and they printed out a card. The hardest part was threading the ribbon through the hole in the card and tying it to the basket, but Fluffy was getting more and more adept with telekinesis.

When daylight came, they said their goodbyes. The police were still cleaning up after the maelstrom of the day before, and the parking lot was cordoned off. Mrs. Moffet employees were able to enter and leave only through the back door, the door that opened onto the street. Fluffy hid among some boxes along the left side of the bakery. She watched as the delivery man came and started grabbing baskets and loading them into his van. Hacker and Mitzi's was among the first. Fluffy waited near the back door until it was left ajar and no one was watching. Then she darted out onto the street, hunkered down behind the tires of a parked car, and waited until nightfall. She wondered if she should've gone home with Hacker and Mitzi. She missed her dad. She missed safety. She had found her poor brother and lost him almost immediately. Now, her only hope was to find Animal U. When it got dark, she started walking toward the mountains. She walked north and west until she found Route 28.

CHAPTER SEVEN — ON THE LAM

Riordan decided to drop in on the one person he knew he could trust: his old college roommate, David Handler. Handler was one of the world's foremost astronomers. He worked out of MIT, where he monitored the world's most powerful telescope, the Galileo, which orbited 500 miles above the Earth. Riordan made his way toward the supertube. As he passed a cash kiosk, he withdrew as much cash as it would allow, $2,000.

Cutting through Haines Park, he tossed his bankcard, along with his handheld, which had a built-in tracking device, into the pond. That's when he heard the footsteps coming up fast behind him. He ran toward the tube station. The footsteps ran too. He figured by the sound it was at least two men. He ran down the long escalator of the station, praying a train would be there to whisk him away from his pursuers, but no. He ducked into the men's room. In one of the stalls, just sitting there, was a homeless man in a long black coat and ratty baseball cap.

"Trade me coats and hats and I'll give you $100," said Riordan.

"Is this gonna get me killed?"

"Not when they see you're not me."

"Okay."

Riordan gave the man the money, and they switched clothing. He could hear a train pulling into the station and the running footsteps. He saw two men run past the restroom, then he pulled the hat over his eyes, and ambled, hunched over, onto the train. His new attire stank like a urinal. This was a local, going in the wrong direction, but at the next stop, he would be able to take another local going back the other way to Frank Koenig Boulevard, where he could change to the JetTrain heading for Boston.

As soon as he got off the local, he dropped the stinking apparel into the nearest trash can. He boarded the JetTrain and took a seat, not near anyone else. He wondered how long it would take to lose the smell. It took approximately fifteen minutes to reach South Station in Boston. He found a cheap hotel in a seedy neighborhood, where he booked a room under the name Percy Kute. He paid in cash.

In the morning, he found a used clothing shop, bought a new old overcoat and found a hat with a broad brim that could conceal his facial features from the surveillance cameras that were everywhere. He then boarded a local that took him under the Charles River to Kendall Square in Cambridge.

When he got to Dr. Handler's office, he was greeted by a stunning example of how the shrinking of the world and the erasure of ethnic and racial barriers had created some very interesting-looking humans. She was a blend of Indian, African and Scottish. She had deep brown skin, black billowing curls, and cornflower blue eyes. She was about forty years old, and she was a knockout. When she opened the door, all Riordan could think was: *If I were only twenty years younger*.

"Hi," said Riordan. "Is Dr. Handler here?"

"No." She scrutinized him suspiciously.

"Do you know when he'll be in?"

"No. We haven't seen Dr. Handler in quite some time." She was clearly nervous and kept looking around at the three surveillance cameras that were mounted around the room near the ceiling and followed their every move. Riordan kept his hat on and covered his eyes.

"I'm his assistant, Indira. Who are you?"

"Oh, I'm an old buddy of Dave's," said Riordan, picking up on her nervousness and intentionally not giving his name. Then he whispered: "Is there someplace we can talk?"

"C'mon," she said and led him down the hall, and into the elevator. "There's a coffee shop across the street. We can talk there."

Once outside, the professor extended his hand. "Jim Riordan, just came up from Kingston."

"Indira Afia Fitzpatrick." They shook hands, but she was still eyeing him suspiciously. "How do you know Dr. Handler?"

"We were roommates in college."

"What college?"

"NYU—before they changed it to Kingston U."

She smiled and breathed a sigh of relief. "Jim Riordan. Yes, he's spoken of you."

They crossed Mass Ave and entered the Coffee Stop. He bought her a mocha latte and a black coffee for himself. They sat down at a small table by the window.

"Dr. Handler's been missing for a month," said Indira. "Some D.I.S. people came around and took all the computers. No one says anything about it. We no longer have access to the Galileo."

"What do you think it's about?"

"I think he saw something—she gestured upward—out *there*."

"Really?"

"There's more: all the major astronomers and astrophysicists on the planet have disappeared."

"What?!"

"It's true."

"How do you know this?"

"Things get around. They can't completely suppress everything and everyone."

"What could he have seen?" mused Riordan.

"I don't know. If I did, I'd be gone too. Whatever it was, it was big...What about you. What brings you to Cambridge?"

"You're not gonna believe this, but the D.I.S. is after me too."

"I believe it."

"They think I'm an animal rights activist."

"Are you?"

"No, but my cat is. I let her leave to join the movement, shot off my big mouth about it in a bar, and now I'm in the soup. I had no idea how serious these guys were."

"They're serious alright. So you're 'on the lam'?"

"Uh, yeah. You like old movies too?"

She smiled, raising an eyebrow. "Yeah." A pause. "So what are you gonna do now?"

"I don't know. I was hoping I could hide out at Dave's place, but I guess that's out."

Indira thought for a moment, giving him an enigmatic half-smile. "You can stay at mine until we figure something out."

"Really? No, I couldn't ask you to do that."

"It's okay. Really. I hate those D.I.S. bastards."

"You live alone?"

"Uh-huh."

Art and his girlfriend, Laura, a petite pretty blonde about twenty-five, arrived at Riordan's apartment, toting his easel and a newly-stretched canvas. The D.I.S. had already come and gone. The basket of muffins and mice sat outside the door, which had been left open by the cops. Apparently, the delivery guy had shown up after the D.I.S., had seen the disarray, dropped the basket and fled. The place had been completely ransacked. The computers were gone, as was Fluffy's tracking collar. Art looked under the doormat. The keycard was still there. "I guess they don't look in the most obvious places," he said, half to himself, half to Laura.

"Look, muffins!" said Laura. Then, "What the hell happened here?"

"I told you," he whispered, "the D.I.S. is after the professor. Watch what you say; the place might be bugged." They dragged in the easel and canvas.

"Wow," said Art, looking around. "He was right; the light is beautiful up here." He set up the easel where the eastern light from the balcony would hit the canvas.

Laura brought the basket inside and set it on the kitchen counter. "Want a muffin?"

"Yeah. Very odd. Now, who would send the professor muffins?"

Laura looked at the card. "There's no sender's name." She started to unwrap the package. Then let out a piercing shriek. "Aaaaahhhhhh, mice!"

Hacker and Mitzi jumped out onto the kitchen counter. "Shhhhh!" said Hacker.

"No screaming, no screaming!" squeaked Mitzi.

There was a sudden dead silence. Art and Laura regarded the mice, slack-jawed.

"They're GABS," said Laura.

"Obviously," said Art. "But how did you do that? How come we can hear you speak? There's no computer..."

"Ya like that?" said Hacker. "I invented it. It's called the voice disk. Y'see these little disks on these collars we're wearin'? I made 'em." Hacker and Mitzi surveyed the apartment. "I guess it's safe to assume you're not the professor."

"That's right. I'm Art, and this is my girlfriend, Laura. The professor asked us to stay here while he's, ahem, out of town..." Art walked around the place, looking under lampshades, picking up objets d'art, looking under ashtrays.

"Have you got a handheld?" asked Hacker. "Yes."

"Can I borrow it for a moment?"

Art put his handheld on the counter near Hacker. Hacker touched the screen a few times with his nose. They watched as an app downloaded. "Okay, pick it up and hit 'Detect'." Art did as he was told. "Your handheld is now a bug detector. If there are any bugs in the room, it will beep like a Geiger counter, faster and faster as it gets closer to the bug."

Art swept the entire apartment and uncovered a total of six tiny hidden microphones, each one no bigger than a watch battery. He flushed them all down the toilet.

"Amazing. Who taught you to do that?"

"We've got to get out of here—*now*. They've already heard too much."

"You're right," said Art. "Get back in the basket. Laura, you take the basket." Art folded up his easel and grabbed the canvas.

"Where are we going?" asked Hacker.

"My loft. It's very nearby. All they know is my first name and Laura's they'll never find out where I live."

"I hope you're right," said Hacker.

As they took the elevator to the garage, D.I.S. agents were taking the other elevator to the 150th floor. Art's van was parked in the fifteen-minute loading zone. He loaded his gear into the van, Laura got in the front seat holding the muffin basket, and they took off. They passed more D.I.S. agents pulling up in their distinctive black unmarked cars on their way out, but no one took notice of them. Art kept checking the rearview mirror.

"Anyone following us?" asked Hacker.

"No, I don't think so."

Art's loft was just blocks away. Once inside, Hacker and Mitzi hopped out of the basket and surveyed the spacious artist's loft.

"Better scan your place too. Can't be too careful," said Hacker.

Art scanned for bugs, but there were no beeps. Then they sat at the table and had muffins.

"So what happened to the professor?" asked Hacker.

Art told Hacker and Mitzi about the incident in the bar, how he had warned the professor, and how the professor had made a hasty departure, apparently just before the D.I.S. had arrived. He told them how the professor wanted to hire Art to do a painting of Fluffy. He showed them the photo.

"Aww, that's so cute. She was younger then," said Mitzi.

"Did Fluffy send you to the professor's place?" asked Art.

"That's right," said Hacker.

"So she's still alive?"

"She was as of this morning. As far as I know, the three of us were the only survivors of the police bombardment of our hideout. Did you see it on the news?"

"We sure did," chimed in Laura. "I work for CNS. In fact, I intercepted a video that was sent to CNS. So far, I'm the only one who's seen it, the only one who knows it exists…"

"Huh? Laura, why didn't you tell me?" said Art, a trifle indignant.

"Art, this is hot stuff. Very hot. Anybody who knows about this is automatically in great danger. You still want to see it?"

Art, Hacker, and Mitzi all responded at once: "Yeah!"

"Okay," said Laura. "Brace yourselves." She took out her handheld, synced it up to the big screen on the wall, and pressed Play.

Janet was filming herself with her handheld. The video was shaky, as was her voice. In the background, you could hear loud explosions. You could see glimpses of Rudy and Giuseppe firing their grenade launchers.

"This is Janet Epps. The GAB animals are not violent. I and I alone blew up the extermination center. The others voted for nonviolence, but my hatred for my father and his hatred for the animals I love, drove me to violate the pact. I didn't know my brother was working in there. I killed him." Here, she breaks down in tears. "I'll be dead in a few minutes, and I'm glad. But don't blame the GABs. They're smarter and better than us. We should learn from them. My father, Jeremiah Epps, is…" You could hear the whistle of the incoming bomb as Janet pressed the Send button.

There was a moment of stunned silence, then… "Holy shit, Laura! How long have you been sitting on this?" said Art.

"It came in day before yesterday when I was screening all the incoming emails to CNS. I could have shown it to my bosses, but I suspect that Epps has them in his pocket and it would never be aired."

"You're right about that," said Art. "But what do we do with it now?"

"I know exactly what to do with it," said Hacker. "We put it up on Z-Tube, Chatify, Spacebook—all of em! This'll go viral worldwide in about ten minutes."

"But what if the D.I.S. traces it back to us?" asked Laura.

"I can post it anonymously. It'll go through five remote servers on three continents. Nobody will be able to figure out who posted it. And then the news services will have to carry it—because it will cause such a stir they won't be able to ignore it. And I've got another idea: make a video of me speaking, as an introduction. We can edit that onto the front of Janet's. I've got a few things I'd like to say to the world."

Laura positioned her handheld to shoot Hacker on the kitchen counter against a plain white wall—no way to identify his whereabouts. "Okay, Hacker, ready, and—action!"

"This is Hacker. As you can hear, I'm a GAB animal with a voice. Soon all GABs will have a device like this one to let their voices be heard by everyone. Janet Epps was a friend of mine, a friend to all animals. She was killed by police under the command of her own father, Jeremiah Epps. Epps has been conducting a systematic campaign to exterminate us. He wants you to believe we are a threat to mankind. That's a lie. We want to help make the world a better place. We don't want to hurt anybody. What you are about to see is a video Janet shot in her last few minutes of life. It speaks for itself. All imprisoned GAB animals must be freed now. We demand equal rights to humans, nothing more, nothing less. Hacker out."

"Cut," said Laura.

"Now, lemme have your handheld," said Hacker. "I'll just edit this onto the front of Janet's, and we're good to go. Janet, the last laugh will be yours... Oh my god, the *bar*!"

"Shit," said Art, "my paintings are hanging in Scully's. I've gotta warn him!" Art started to dial Scully.

"Now, hold on," said Hacker. "What if they're already monitoring Scully?"

"You're right. They probably are. That's where that D.I.S. guy overheard our conversation."

"Take me over there," said Hacker. "Mitzi, you stay here with Laura. We'll be back soon." Then to Art. "Take a pencil and a small pad of paper."

Art put Hacker, the pad, and pencil in his pockets and walked toward Scully's.

"What're we gonna do?" asked Art.

"Will he even be open?" asked Hacker.

"Yeah. He opens at eleven a.m. Should just be opening now."

"Good, the place will probably be empty…"

When Art entered Scully's, he put his finger to his lips, telling Scully to keep silent. As they hoped, there were no customers. Art took out the pad and wrote:

YOUR PLACE IS PROBABLY BUGGED. THE PROFESSOR'S IN TROUBLE. HE WAS FOLLOWED HOME FROM HERE. TAKE ALL MY PAINTINGS DOWN AND BURN THEM. GET RID OF MY BUSINESS CARD AND ANYTHING YOU HAVE CONNECTING YOU TO ME, INCLUDING THIS NOTE. IF ANYBODY ASKS YOU ABOUT ME, YOU KNOW NOTHING, OKAY?

Scully nodded, clearly unnerved. Art wrote: NICE KNOWIN' YA and calmly walked out of there.

On the walk back, Art asked Hacker: "Is there any way you can find out if they have my handheld tapped?"

"As a matter of fact, there is," said Hacker.

When they got back to Art's place, Hacker asked Art for his handheld. He dialed a number. After three rings, he heard a series of beeps. "You're clean," said Hacker.

Chief Davis looked solemn. More than solemn; anguished. "Mr. Epps, I have some very painful news to tell you."

"What is it?" said Epps.

"The forensic reports have come in from the warehouse explosion on Cumpston Street."

"So?"

"One of the bodies was that of your daughter, Janet Epps. I wanted to tell you before you heard it on the news."

Epps sat silent for a long moment. His eyes teared up. His jaw clenched tight. His lip quivered. "Make sure it does NOT get on the news, Mr. Davis."

Davis looked at the floor. "Yes, sir."

"You can go now, Mr. Davis. Thank you."

Davis left Epps's office, closing the door behind him. Epps slumped forward onto the desk, burying his face in his arms, and wept.

CHAPTER EIGHT — INTO THE WOODS

The Catskills were an old, worn-down mountain range. Not high and pointy like the Rockies or the Himalayas, but rolling, rounded hills, humbled by time and glaciers. Long ago, these mountains used to be a vacation destination for city dwellers looking to escape the summer heat. There were sprawling hotels, bungalow colonies, and busy towns. But now the world was cooling, and those with means could take themselves to the Rockies or the Swiss Alps, or anywhere on Earth for that matter in an hour or so. And those without means had no jobs from which to take vacations. So, the Catskills had been surrendered back into the arms of nature and were once again magnificent.

Fluffy walked and walked. She followed the road called Route 28 but walked alongside the road, about twenty-five feet into the woods, using her "stealth walk," crouching below the tall weeds, while moving her little feet fast and silent.

Although hundreds of years old, Route 28 was still a two-lane winding mountain road, which grew gradually steeper as Fluffy walked on. She walked on the left side of the road with the oncoming traffic headed towards her. Occasionally a car would go whooshing by, kicking up a blast of wind and dry leaves in its wake. The almost-full moon made the night very bright and Fluffy saw many creatures darting to and fro in the woods off to her left. She saw raccoons, possums, and squirrels. She heard the hoot of an owl and remembered that Hacker had told her they hunted by night and were capable of swooping down and carrying off even a cat of her size. But she passed unmolested. A seductive profusion of smells emanated from the woods, beckoning Fluffy to come in but she resisted her curiosity and erred on the side of caution. After walking for several hours, she was very hungry and tired.

She came at last to a roadside rest stop for motorists. There were restrooms and wooden picnic tables, a water fountain, and places for six vehicles to park. Under and around the tables, Fluffy found some scraps of food, which she devoured, not caring how repulsive they were. She leaped into the water fountain and pressed the metal button with her mind, causing it to come to life. She was very thirsty. Drinking the running water reminded her of being at home, where she would jump into the sink and her dad would run the water for her to drink. Thinking of this made her sad. Sad and tired; not just physically, but tired of being afraid. She decided to rest under one of the tables.

After maybe thirty minutes, a car pulled in and parked. It was a very old car with only ground capabilities. A mother and two young children got out and entered the restrooms. The mother and little girl went into the women's and the little boy, who was older, maybe eight, entered the men's. Fluffy guessed from their shabby appearance that they were rips that had gotten out of one of the ripcoms. She decided to try something risky. When they came out, she was sitting in the middle of the empty parking lot, mewing pathetically.

"Look, Mommy, a kitty!" cried the little girl. She was about five.

"Hey, it's wearing a collar," said the boy. He ran over and reached for Fluffy's voice disc. "It's a Miniblaster! I want one of these!"

"Don't touch that... please," said Fluffy.

The boy jumped back as if he'd stuck his finger in an electrical socket. "It spoke!"

"Are you GAB?" asked the mother.

"Yes. My name is Fluffy. What's yours?"

"My name's Tommy," volunteered the boy. "Are you a terrorist?"

"Don't be silly," said Fluffy. "GABs are not terrorists. Some bad people spread that rumor so everyone would hate us."

"But how can you speak without a computer?" asked the woman.

"This thing that looks like a Miniblaster, it's a new invention that enables me to speak out loud."

"Are you lost?"

"Not exactly. I'm trying to get to West Kill Falls. Are you going there?"

"Not all the way, but we can give you a ride part way," said the woman.

"Thank you," said Fluffy.

The woman opened the back door, and Fluffy hopped in. "I wanna sit in back with Fluffy!" said the boy.

"No, I wanna sit in back!" cried the girl.

The woman, an average-looking white woman around thirty-five with too many lines on her face and a cut on her lip, sighed. "Okay, you can both sit in the back with Fluffy." The kids piled in and sat on either side of Fluffy and petted her incessantly. The woman started the car, and they were on their way. Fluffy put up with all the pawing, happy to be getting a lift.

"Why are you going to West Kill Falls?" asked the boy.

"I can't tell you that. All I can say is, there are people who want to hurt me, and I'm trying to find a place where I'll be safe." Fluffy had never learned how to lie.

"We're trying to be safe too," said the little girl. "Daddy socked Momma in the mouth."

"So we're running away to Grandma's," said the boy.

"Children!" cried the mother. "I told you never to speak of this to anyone."

"Now you have my secret and I have yours," said Fluffy. "Let's never give our secrets away, okay?"

"Okay," said the kids together.

After about a half-hour the woman stopped the car. There was an old mailbox that marked a dirt road, heading off to the right. "This is where we turn off," said the woman.

"This is the road to Grandma's house," said Tommy.

"Would you like to come with us, Fluffy? I'll bet you're hungry," said the woman.

"Well, yes, I am rather hungry," said Fluffy.

"Please come," said the little girl.

"Yeah, we can play games," said Tommy.

"Well...okay," said Fluffy. "But I have to leave first thing tomorrow."

"Yay!" cheered the kids.

Grandma's house was an ancient wooden cottage deep in the woods, with the paint peeling off, about a mile off the main road. When she heard the car pull up, Grandma came out to greet her family. Fluffy heard a big dog barking from the back of the house.

Grandma was a gray-haired old lady who looked at least seventy, although, looking at her daughter, Fluffy guessed she was probably quite a bit younger. She wore glasses (a rarity), a faded floral print dress, and antiquated black old lady shoes. She hugged her grandchildren, then her daughter. Then she regarded Fluffy.

"And who have we got here?" she said.

"This is Fluffy," said Tommy.

"She's GAB," said the woman significantly.

"Oh, GAB. So you can understand everything we say?"

"Oh yes," said Fluffy.

Grandma was startled. "How did you do that?"

"It's a new invention," said Tommy. "That thing around her neck."

"We picked up Fluffy hitchhiking, you might say," said the woman. "She's very hungry."

"Well, you've come to the right place," said Grandma. "Come right this way, Fluffy. We'll get you something yummy to eat." As they all entered the house, the woman whispered something in her mother's ear. Grandma led Fluffy to the kitchen, which was in the back of the house. Just outside the kitchen door was the backyard where the big dog was barking furiously and scratching at the door to get in.

"You're not going to let him in here, are you?" said Fluffy.

"Oh, don't worry," said Grandma. "That's just Brutus. His bark is worse than his bite."

"Just the same…"

"Don't worry, Fluffy, we won't let him in."

She opened a can of some very smelly meat. Fluffy guessed that it was some kind of dog food. Grandma spooned out a generous portion into a bowl and bustled about the kitchen a bit more before putting it and a bowl of water on the floor for Fluffy. Fluffy didn't like the smell of it, but she was hungry enough to eat a horse—and she suspected that was exactly what she was doing.

The family left Fluffy alone in the kitchen while she ate, and Grandma showed them to their rooms upstairs. After she finished eating, a great wave of tiredness came over her. Her vision got blurry, then everything went black.

When Fluffy regained consciousness, it was daytime. At first, she had no idea where she was, then the previous night started to come back to her. As her eyes began to focus, she realized she was in a wire cage, the kind in which people keep large snakes or hamsters. Fluffy could smell several different previous animal occupants. A terrible jolt of fear passed through her. The cage appeared to be in a spare room downstairs. There were a small cot and some boxes and old clothes. It smelled musty and stale. Why had these people imprisoned her? What were they planning to do? She didn't have to wait long to find out. At length, Grandma entered. "Sorry, Fluffy, but you know, there's a hefty reward for runaway GABs. We're not rich people," she said, "so we gotta do what we gotta do. My daughter will be driving you back to the city after breakfast."

"No, please!" cried Fluffy. But Grandma had already left the room. There was a big padlock on the cage. Fluffy tried to pick it telekinetically, but she had no experience in this area, and it was futile. She knew if she didn't get out of here now she was doomed. Then Tommy, the little boy, entered the room softly, quietly.

"I'm not supposed to be in here," he whispered. "I have the key to that lock."

"Are you going to set me free, Tommy?"

"On one condition: I want that Miniblaster."

"Okay," said Fluffy.

Tommy unlocked the cage door. In a split second, Fluffy plunged through it, nearly knocking Tommy over, streaked across the room, and leaped out the half-open window.

"Sorry, Tommy, I need this," she called as she disappeared into the woods. Then, under her breath, "Dad was right; humans *are* scum." Fluffy found her way back to the dirt road that led to Route 28. She was sure that, in a few minutes, she would hear the barking of that awful dog and know they were on her trail. Then it occurred to her that they might come after her in the car. She followed the road but ran alongside it a few feet into the woods. Fortunately, Tommy had not confessed to setting her free for at least ten minutes. That gave her the head start she needed to make it to the main road, turn north, and keep running.

She had to run on the right side of the road now because on the left side was a precipitous drop. She stayed in the tall grass beside the road. Soon she heard the clunky sound of the old car coming up behind her. Without looking, she knew it was them. She crouched down in the grass and froze, praying they would pass her by. They went by slowly, then stopped a few yards ahead. Then the back door opened and out came Brutus. He sniffed the air, picked up her scent and, barking enthusiastically, took off running, straight for Fluffy. Fluffy gasped and ran into the woods. She ran for all she was worth. Brutus stayed right behind her, and by his barking, she could tell he was getting closer. She began to give up hope. She was getting very tired, and this dog would surely kill her when he caught her. Then an idea came to her. A very dangerous idea, but the only one she could think of.

She reached a hollow log and, instead of jumping over it, she jumped up on it and wheeled around to face Brutus. She sat majestically, doing her damnedest to quell the fear that raged inside her. The dog came charging out of the brush, and when he was only five feet away, she said in her most commanding Katharine Hepburn voice, "Stop, Brutus!" And Brutus stopped and cocked his head, looking at her with an uncertain whine. "Sit, Brutus!" Brutus sat. "Now, lie down!" Brutus lay down. "Now, stay. Stay, Brutus. Stay!" Calmly, Fluffy turned her back on the dog, and casually trotted off into the woods. After a minute, she looked back. Brutus was still obediently prone. As soon as she was out of his sight, she took off at top speed and didn't look back. Up ahead she could hear the sound of a babbling brook. She decided to find it and follow it up the mountain. Maybe this was the stream that led to West Kill Falls.

When she reached it, she realized she was very thirsty and decided to take a drink. It was the sweetest, coolest, freshest water she had ever tasted; so different from the stuff that came out of taps in the city. Her senses were inundated with the sounds and smells of the forest. *This is the way it should be*, she thought. And then she remembered her dream—the one with the wolf. She looked around nervously for a moment, but no sign of predators. *Humans have really messed up this world*. She began the walk upstream. She followed a trail alongside the stream that had been blazed by generations of animals coming here to drink. She walked for many hours, constantly coming across new and exciting smells and sights. She saw some deer and even a bear. She wondered what it would be like to give in to her natural instincts: to hunt, to stalk and kill and eat something, a bird or even a... but no. After getting to know Hacker and Mitzi, the idea of killing and eating a mouse had become unthinkable to her. So, this was the blessing—and the curse—of human thought: The loss of one's natural instincts, the acquisition of empathy, and paradoxically, the loss of innocence.

After several hours, it began to get dark. The weather was clear and, when the full moon rose, it lit up the forest like daytime. And that's when she heard the howling.

Wolves, she thought. But then she remembered. Hacker said they were coyotes. Just as bad. Maybe worse. It sounded like dozens of them howling and yipping, off in the distance. She hurried along her way, still following the stream.

Then, out of the corner of her eye, she saw something move alongside her, on the far side of the stream, about fifty feet off to the right. It was a large animal, like a skinny dog. Then came a rustling off to her left. Another one. Behind her, she sensed two more. Fluffy broke into a full run, and the coyotes kept right up with her. Now they were very close; four of them, closing fast. The adrenalin of fear took over and she ran faster and faster. Then, suddenly, she felt the teeth on her tail, and she was jerked up short, hanging by her tail in midair. She jackknifed her body, claws extended and scratched at the creature's face. It dropped her, but the others were moving in for the kill. Fluffy said a silent goodbye to the world. All of a sudden there was a yellow shaft of light coming from straight ahead. A huge dog charged out of a doorway barking ferociously, fangs bared. "Get away from her!" he said in a familiar voice, a voice that was inside Fluffy's head. The coyotes fled.

"Bernard?"

Then someone picked her up and brought her inside the cabin. Fluffy was bleeding profusely and was getting a little woozy. She thought she saw Jack, Tigger, and Bernard and some of the other animals she had liberated from the extermination center, but she assumed it must be a hallucination.

Then a beautiful lady was leaning over her. She was old, with long straight hair that was pure white. She had deep blue eyes that radiated kindness. Her face was not old, but not young. It was a face that was somehow timeless and unchanging. "Just relax, Fluffy," she said. "You're safe now." Her lips did not move. Her voice was inside Fluffy's head. She had an electric razor, and she shaved the fur off the base of Fluffy's tail where the wounds were. Beside her stood her assistant, a brown-skinned woman in her fifties. "This is Clara. She will take care of you," said the beautiful lady. Clara poured antiseptic on the wounds, and then she gave Fluffy a shot of something that made her tail go numb, and it made her go to sleep as well.

When she awoke, Fluffy thought perhaps she had died. She looked around at her friends from the hideout, whom she assumed were dead, and then there was this angelic-looking woman standing over her. Her tail had a bandage on it, a sure sign she was not dead. "You'll be alright in a few days," the lady said.

"Where am I?" asked Fluffy.

"You're in my cabin. I'm Angelica. The animals call me Mama Angelica."

"Jack, is that really you?" Fluffy was overcome with emotion.

"It's me, Fluffy."

"And Tigger, Bernard. How can you be alive? How did you get here?"

"I missed the jump across the rooftops and landed in a dumpster," said Tigger. "But I landed on my feet, and only bruised my paw a little. Then I remembered to find Route 28, and I did. I got lucky. I jumped into the back of a truck, and it took me almost all the way here. I wandered into the woods, found the stream and followed it."

"How did you get out, Bernard?"

Jack told Fluffy the story. Bernard had led Jack, the other cat, Sally, who was a short-haired tabby, and the two dogs—Stella, a small, black, mixed-breed with mottled fur that stuck out in all directions and Leroy, a pug—to a large drain in the floor of the bathroom at the hideout. He'd levitated the heavy cover off the drain and they had all managed to crawl through the drain pipe to a bigger sewer pipe, which eventually led them to a manhole. Bernard knew of a certain diner, a truck stop, where there were truckers who were sympathetic to the GAB cause, sort of an Underground Railroad. There, all the animals were hosed off (they were smelling a bit ripe after the trip through the sewer pipes), put into boxes, loaded onto a truck, and driven straight here.

"Bernard, you've been here before?" asked Fluffy.

"Oh yes," said Bernard, "but it's a long story, and you should get some rest now."

"But you've got to tell me one thing," said Fluffy, fighting exhaustion.

"Yes?"

"How did you come to be in the extermination center? Were you captured?"

"No. I walked in through the out-door, you might say."

"Huh?"

"When all the non-GABs ran out, I walked in, got in line with the other GABs, and joined your group."

"But why were you there in the first place?"

"I was tracking you, Fluffy. When you got involved with the resistance, I was afraid something would happen to you. I was hoping to get you out of there sooner, but one can never predict how things will unfold. You know those psychic flashes you've been getting about Animal U? They came from me. I'm the Dean of Students and Professor of Special Powers at Animal U. We've had our eyes on a few exceptional animals for a while now, and you're one of them."

"But—"

"Now that's enough for one night," said Mama Angelica. "Let's all get some sleep. In the morning, we leave for Animal U."

Fluffy fell asleep imagining how it would be at Animal U. She could hear the lovely sound of falling water; West Kill Falls was very near.

CHAPTER NINE — THE SECRET VALLEY

The next morning Mama Angelica and all the animals left the cabin. Clara stayed behind, ready to receive any other GAB refugees that found their way to the cabin. When Fluffy saw it from the outside in daylight, she realized why she hadn't been able to see it last night. Mama Angelica's cabin was made of dark brown wood, the color of tree bark, and it was covered with green leafy vines. With the blackout curtains drawn, no one would be able to see it in the woods at night. They walked along the footpath beside the steam in the direction of the falls, which were just around the next bend.

"My ancestors were among the first Dutch settlers in this region," said Mama Angelica. "My family used to own all of this land, and the Secret Valley as well."

"Secret Valley?" said Fluffy.

"Yes. That's where Animal U is, on the site of our family estate."

"But why is it secret?"

"You'll see."

Just then, 100 feet upstream, West Kill Falls came into view. It was a small waterfall as waterfalls go, but magically beautiful. The water flowed beneath a narrow footbridge at the top, and cascaded down a staircase of moss-covered rocks, each maybe three or four feet high. The whole thing wasn't more than twenty feet in height.

And on that footbridge, there they were: the mother of the two little kids, Grandma wielding a shotgun, and Brutus, barking and growling for all he was worth.

"So, I see you brought some friends with ya, eh, Fluffy?" said Grandma, training the shotgun on the group.

"Who are these people, Fluffy?" asked Mama Angelica telepathically.

"The younger one gave me a ride. I'm sorry. I told her I was looking for the falls. They drugged me and locked me in a cage. They were going to turn me in for a reward."

"Well, we haven't got enough room in the car for that big dog, but I bet we can get the rest of you in the trunk. Now, all of you just climb on up here to Grandma."

"Or what?" said Mama Angelica. "You're going to shoot us?"

"Oh, and look—they got themselves a human friend. Yeah, that's right, sister. I'll shoot ya all and not bat an eyelash. There might be a reward for some of ya dead *or* alive."

Bernard looked at the shotgun. It began to get hot. In seconds it was glowing red.

Grandma dropped it, shaking her scalded hands. "Owww! What the hell...?"

Then the shotgun raised itself up off the bridge, aimed itself at Grandma and her daughter, and cocked itself. The three bounty hunters took off running, and Bernard tossed the shotgun into the stream.

Completely unfazed, Mama Angelica put the hood up on her raincoat. "Look out, we're going to get wet," she said. Bernard led the way, crossing the stream by stepping from stone to stone. Fluffy followed; then Jack, Tigger, Stella, Leroy, and Sally. Mama Angelica brought up the rear, giving the smaller animals a boost as they climbed the slippery mossy steps on the far side of the falls. They followed Bernard under the falls and disappeared into what seemed to be a dark cave. Mama Angelica had to enter on her hands and knees; the ceiling was no more than four feet high. Bernard looked at what appeared to be a solid rock wall at the back of the cave and it began to move. A cleft opened up as the massive rock split in two. The two halves pivoted and opened like a gate. Mama Angelica took out her flashlight and led the way. Once inside, the ceiling got higher and she was able to stand up. She ushered all the animals into the tunnel, and when everyone was in, the rock gate closed. "This tunnel's about a mile long," said Mama Angelica, and they began the trek. The tunnel was solid granite on all sides, but the floor was dirt.

"How was this tunnel made?" asked Fluffy.

"No one really knows. It was used by the Indians before my ancestors came to this country," said Mama Angelica. Then she whispered, "There is actually a secret panel that an ordinary person can press to make the gates open, but Bernard likes to impress the newcomers with his powers."

The tunnel snaked through the heart of West Kill Mountain and, after what seemed like hours, they came to another solid rock wall. Bernard willed the rocks to part and, like the entrance, the gate slowly swung open, revealing a sight rarely seen by man or beast. A verdant valley spread below them, rolling fields dotted with fruit trees and wildflowers, and in the middle, an elegant estate with a great manor house, shade trees, and many outbuildings, spreading out in all directions. There were barns and sheds and dwellings. It looked like a little village. Fluffy recognized the main house at once as the manor house depicted in her visions. To Fluffy, this was literally a dream come true, but the reality was even more beautiful than her dreams.

CHAPTER TEN — LOVE AND THE BIG ROCK

James Riordan was feeling surprisingly euphoric for a man being hunted by the police. It was a glorious Saturday in May, warm and sunny. Because of the many surveillance cameras mounted on buildings and light poles, Riordan still wore his broad-brimmed hat and a pair of dark glasses as he and Indira strolled along Mass Ave near Harvard Square. The art renaissance had spawned a cornucopia of galleries, performance spaces, and outdoor venues where choral groups and improv troupes performed for free on the street. At some point she had taken his arm and he couldn't remember the last time he had strolled arm-in-arm with a beautiful woman. They had just seen an early screening of *Random Harvest* at the Brattle Theater, one of the last brick-and-mortar movie houses still standing.

"Were people really that beautiful and romantic?" Indira was still wiping tears from her eyes.

"Maybe not in real life, but in the movies, yes. I tear up every time I see it," said Riordan. "I guess it's one of the most romantic movies of all time. By today's standards, most would call it absurdly melodramatic, but I don't consider myself to be a man of these times."

All the way down Mass Ave, all Riordan could talk about was Fluffy. He wanted to make Indira see her as he did: brilliant, beautiful, compassionate, perceptive—far superior to him in so many ways. He spoke as any proud father would of his prodigal child. Riordan had a lot of factual knowledge—libraries worth of books—stored in his head, but Fluffy had something Riordan could never have: a luminous soul.

"Your soul is luminous, Jimmy," she said, turning to him. "All souls are. We just need to find our luminosity."

"You're luminous," he said, looking straight into her eyes.

She gave him a look that made Riordan dare to hope. Was she sending signals? Was he imagining it? *Be careful, there's no fool like an old fool*, he thought.

Indira's apartment was on Green Street, a few blocks from the MIT campus. It was about a mile and a half from Harvard Square, but they had walked it without even noticing the distance. Inside was a sanctuary, pervaded by her calm and steady essence. The walls of the small living room were adorned with prints from the Kama Sutra, William Blake, Tibetan Thangkas, and Maxfield Parish. She had painted the spotless, polished wood floor glossy black to cover the years of wear it had endured. There was a small Persian area rug, a low table with cushions, a couch, many plants, and a flatscreen opposite the couch, above the desk and computer. One wall was completely covered by a bookcase, containing dozens of books—actual physical books—on many subjects. The two tandem windows looked out on a small garden in the back of the building. Outside of them was an ancient fire escape which held more plants. This one-bedroom hideaway was minuscule compared to Riordan's palatial condo in Kingston, but to him, Indira's domain was a paradise without equal.

He had been sleeping on her couch for three days now, and what had started out as a nightmare now unfolded as a beautiful dream he could never have anticipated. But what his next move should be he had yet to determine.

"Can you get me access to a phone, a business line, with no connection to either of us?" he asked her.

"We could sneak into my building at night and use one in somebody else's office."

"Yeah, that would be good. I have to get in touch with Art. He's the artist who's staying at my house. I have to know if he's heard from Fluffy."

"Can it wait until Monday? If I'm seen entering the building after hours on a Saturday night, it'll arouse suspicion."

"Sure. So we have tonight and tomorrow to do anything we want. Where would you like to eat dinner?"

"You're going to run out of money. Let me cook for you."

"I don't want to put you to any trouble."

"It'll be my pleasure. I never get to show off my culinary skills. Prepare to be impressed!"

Mark this moment, Riordan said to himself, *for this night, you are truly happy*.

Jeremiah Epps poured another drink for Dr. Handler and refilled his own glass. Epps was three sheets to the wind and Handler dumped most of his drink into the potted palm. They were seated—or rather Handler was seated and Epps was sprawled—on two decadently comfortable silver panné velvet couches opposite each other, with a marble coffee table between, and potted plants book-ending each couch. Epps's vast living room was all white and silver: White plush carpeting, white furniture, a white grand piano, and the silver velvet couches, divans, and big round cushions that floated among the coffee tables and plants. Epps didn't know or care anything about interior decorating. It was Lorna who had it done this way, and Epps kept it like a shrine to her memory. At one end of the room, the architect Fuller had designed a wall fifty feet high made of unpolished granite stones, into which was carved a Mayan-like bas-relief. At the base was a fireplace big enough for a man to walk in.

Epps's estate was situated on a huge swath of wooded hills and rolling fields not far north of Kingston. His grounds were guarded by a small army of human and robot security forces with robot attack dogs that patrolled the grounds, day and night.

"It's such a pleasure to have you as my guest, Dave. May I call you Dave?"

"Sure," said Handler, with an absence of enthusiasm that was lost on Epps.

Handler was a tall, lanky guy, about sixty, with thinning black hair that was turning gray, dark eyes and olive skin.

"You have no idea how simulating—er, stimulating—it is for me to be in the company of someone who is my equal for a change—intellectually, that is."

"Mr. Epps—"

"Call me Jerry."

"Jerry, can I ask you something?"

"Anything!"

"Why am I being held prisoner here?"

"'Prisoner' is such an ugly word, Dave. Can't you think of yourself as my guest?"

"Okay, why am I your unwilling guest?"

"But surely you must know the answer to that." Handler keeps silent. "The asteroid? You and a small handful of other scientists know of its existence, and what it's going to do. If I let you blab it to the world, there will be a general panic, and that will interfere with my plans."

"And what, may I ask, are your plans?"

"I and a few friends are getting out of here. We found a planet with a breathable atmosphere and water that's within striking distance."

"You mean Gliese 667 Cc?"

"Yes. But I'm renaming it Epsilon. Has a better ring, don't you think? We can get there in under fifty years."

"You have an interstellar spacecraft that will go half the speed of light?"

"That's right, up on Moonbase. We've been working on this for many years. The Triumvirate has developed what you might call a contingency plan, for just such an occasion as this."

"How many people can you evacuate?"

"30,000: about all the professionals and the elites that work for the Triumvirate and the important politicians, scientists and artists—you included, of course. Two cargo ships have already departed, loaded with building and agricultural supplies…"

"But Mr.—er, Jerry—in fifty years you and I will be dead. We'll never get there."

"We'll all be in a state of cryogenic suspended animation. We won't age a day."

"You have that technology?"

"Mmm hmm."

"But what about the other two point five billion people?"

Epps made a big exploding sound with his mouth and slowly expanded his hands, palms out, a planet blowing apart. Then he put on an innocent little boy face, smiled and shrugged.

There was a knock at the door. "Yes, what is it?" said Epps.

Hobson, his Chief of Security, stuck his head in the door. "Mr. Epps?"

"Yes, what?" said Epps impatiently.

"There's something on the web I think you need to see."

"What is it?"

"I think you better take a look for yourself, sir."

"Okay, come in, Hobson," said Epps.

"Maybe I'd better…" said Handler, starting to get up.

"No, you can stay."

Hobson entered and lowered the flatscreen from its hiding place in the ceiling. He pressed some buttons on the screen of his handheld. "It's gone viral worldwide on Z-Tube," he said, and Janet's video came on, with Hacker's introduction. A stunned silence.

Then Epps, barely maintaining his composure said, "How did this get out?"

"We don't know. It was posted anonymously, and we can't trace it."

"Well, have it taken down—and trace it!" Epps yelled. "I want you to get the person or thing that posted this!"

"It's already on all the news services."

"Just do it!"

"Yes, sir." Hobson departs. Epps breaks down crying.

"They killed my children, Dave. Those dirty animals killed my children!"

"Errm, that's not precisely true, Jerry," said Handler gently. "Janet killed your son—by accident of course—and she was killed by..."

"It's all because of those animals," said Epps very loudly, cutting him off. "And before I leave this planet I'm going to wipe out every last one of 'em."

"Why bother?" said Handler. "The Earth only has another month, and then—" He made an exploding noise with his mouth and expanded his hands, palms out. But Epps was passed out on the couch opposite him. Then Handler noticed that Epps's handheld had fallen out of his pocket and onto the floor. Handler picked it up and sent a text to Indira: "Being held at Epps estate. Heavy security. Asteroid will destroy Earth in 30 days. Dave." He confirmed that it was sent, then deleted it from Epps's cache.

Indira and Riordan were on her couch watching the news. They were barely paying attention. Riordan had only consumed one drink but was high just being in her company. He couldn't allow himself to believe she could actually be attracted to him, but there was no mistaking her warmth as she snuggled up on the couch. Then the anchor woman's voice caught their attention:

"Epsilon CEO Jeremiah Epps has been in seclusion and incommunicado since the deaths of his two children, twenty-year-old Lucien Epps and twenty-six-year-old Janet Epps." Then Janet's video with Hacker's introduction came on. Riordan and Indira watched in mute fascination. "Janet was killed Wednesday in a shootout with police while defending a GAB terrorist hideout. Lucien was killed when these same terrorists blew up the West Kingston Animal Detention Center late Sunday night. Epsilon media spokesperson Aurora

Malvolio-Jones issued a brief statement, only saying that Epsilon's Senior Vice President of Operations, Valerie Trump, will take temporary command of the company in Epps's absence. Neither Epps nor Trump could be reached for comment.'"

"Epps is an evil creep," said Riordan. "Still, you have to feel sorry for the poor bugger. I hope Fluffy wasn't involved in any of that."

At that moment, Indira's handheld buzzed. It was Handler's text. When she read it, Indira sat bolt upright.

"What is it?" said Riordan. She showed him Handler's message.

"So that's what he saw," she said. For a moment they sat in numbed silence. At last Riordan said, "But, can't they do something? Blow it up? Nuke it?"

"Yeah, that's what they always do in all those movies where an asteroid is about to destroy the Earth," said Indira. "But, if this thing is big enough, we could blow it to pieces and the pieces would still be big enough to destroy the Earth. So, Epps has got Dave and I guess the other scientists held captive. He must have something up his sleeve. He's deliberately keeping the news from getting out. Doesn't want a worldwide panic, I suppose."

"So this is the way the world ends. Not with a whimper but a bang... Couldn't they set off a bomb near it and knock it off course?"

"I don't know, Jimmy. Maybe we better ask Dave."

"Ask Dave?"

"Yeah. We need to get him out of there."

"Huh? Oh, no, not me. I'm no action hero."

"Just calm down and use your brain. I once heard that Epps flies himself to work every day in his private robocopter."

"Yeah, but the news just said..."

"Oh, right. Damn it!"

"Why?"

"Well, just for the hell of it let me do a little research." She grabbed her handheld and, inside of two minutes, she showed him an article, an interview with Epps, dated just a few months earlier. "Look at this: 'Mr. Epps flies himself to work every day in his private robocopter.'"

"But he's not coming to work, they said."

"He's gotta come sometime." She went back to her handheld. "This is it!" she said excitedly. She showed him an article: JEREMIAH EPPS SLATED TO MAKE KEYNOTE SPEECH AT ROBOTICS CONFERENCE JUNE 7th

"June seventh. That's Thursday. The conference is in the Epsilon Building. He's gotta be there for that—and MIT Robotics will be sending a team with their latest gadget. I have a friend on that team!" said Indira.

"Okay," said Riordan cautiously. "So what's your plan?"

"So what if we were able to get on that roof and into his robocopter when no one was looking."

"Yeah?" Riordan was beginning to get interested.

"We stow away in his robocopter and just wait for him to fly us to his house."

"Oh, right. And then he just invites us in for some tea and crumpets..."

"No. We stick a gun in his back and make him get us in, get Dave, and get us out. We keep him with us, so they don't shoot down the copter, and we fly off."

"To where?"

"What, I have to think of everything?"

"Yes."

They both smile. It's been years since Riordan has smiled like that, or seen anyone smile at him like that. *Typical. I find love, and the world ends*.

"So, where are you gonna get a gun? said Riordan.

"I have one."

"A real gun?"

"A real gun.

"But that is so illegal."

"My ex was a cop. He left it here. Wanted me to be safe."

"Oh god, what am I getting into?"

"Hey. What have we got to lose, right?"

"Being as we're all doomed, I suppose you're right. But what about security? Don't they have a metal detector in that building? We'll never get a gun in there. Let's just forget it."

"Dave's our only chance to stop the world from ending, and you say 'forget it'?" Riordan looked sheepish. They sat and thought about it.

"My friend Bobby is the lead designer at MIT robotics. I'll get him to get us in."

"And the gun? Don't they X-ray all the gadgets?"

Indira thought for a long moment. "Let me talk to Bobby. He's very quirky; a nerd, but cool. I think he can be trusted."

Monday morning, Indira went to work as usual. She called Bobby and asked if he was free for lunch. They met at the Good & Healthy on Mass Ave. Indira looked grave. Bobby was a skinny guy in his twenties who looked and dressed like a twentieth-century punk rocker: head shaved on one side with long green hair on the other, multiple piercings, tattoos, black leather jacket. The department head took a dim view of his image, but what could he do? Bobby was the best robotics engineer on the planet.

"Indira, what's going on? Where's that eternally-cheery disposition?"

"Bobby, I have something very, very important and very, very secret I need to discuss with you. You have to promise me that this conversation will never go beyond the two of us."

"Okay, I promise."

She laid out the whole thing to Bobby: the text from Dave, the asteroid, and her plan to kidnap Epps and free Dave.

All Bobby could say was, "My god, my god. There was so much more I wanted to do."

"Don't despair yet, Bobby. Right now, Dave's our only hope."

"So what do you need from me?"

As it turns out, Bobby was the designer of the new robopet

commissioned by Epsilon, and they would be demonstrating it at the conference.

"Her name is Penelope," he confided gleefully, "and she's a completely lifelike little pony. Perfect for a rich, spoiled little girl who's always wanted a pony, but whose rich, spoiled parents don't want to have to feed, house and clean up after a real one. So, here's what I was thinking..."

Bobby told Indira that he could get Team MIT IDs and coveralls for her and Riordan, and how they could conceal the gun: He would line Penelope's hind quarters with a thin layer of lead foil, impenetrable to X-rays. Penelope was almost completely anatomically correct. She even had an anal cavity under her tail.

"So we stick the gun..."

"That's right. Up the horsie's ass!" He accompanied this with the appropriate gesture. Indira and Bobby cackled madly at the notion.

When Indira told Riordan the plan that evening, they both rolled with laughter. "Brilliant, positively brilliant!" said Riordan. He grabbed her and hugged her, they turned toward each other, and they kissed. It was a long and wonderful kiss—the best Riordan had ever had—and in the face of their impending doom, they were happy.

"Time to find that telephone," said Riordan.

"Okay, let's go."

Riordan finished his drink, Indira took her key card, and they walked to the building where she worked. She let them in and they found an unlocked office on the ground floor. Riordan picked up a desk phone and dialed Art's number. After a few rings, Art answered.

"Hello?"

"Art, it's Jim Riordan."

"Professor!"

"Any news of Fluffy?"

"Yes. She's alive, or at least she was as of a few days ago. As a matter of fact, we have a couple of friends of hers here. Hacker and Mitzi. They're mice."

"You're kidding."

"No. the smartest mice you, or I, or anyone has ever met. Fluffy was part of their GAB resistance group. After their hideout got blown up, they and Fluffy wound up in a bakery close by. They had themselves delivered to your apartment in a basket of muffins. Fluffy's on her way to Animal U. It's on West Kill Mountain, near West Kill Falls."

"Are you sure your phone is safe?"

"Yes. Hacker checked my phone and the D.I.S. doesn't know about me."

"Now listen, Art. Something very big is happening. Earth-shattering, you might say. I can't explain now, but can you get a car and drive those mice up to West Kill Falls?"

"Yes, I think so."

"Good. Meet me up there Thursday night about this time."

"Okay—" Art sounded rather tentative.

"It's important, Art. Be there." And he hung up. That night Riordan no longer slept on the couch.

CHAPTER ELEVEN — ANIMAL U

For Fluffy, the first stop was the infirmary, formerly a guest house, a few yards from the main house. "We have to change those bandages," Mama Angelica explained. "They got all wet when you passed under the falls."

Mama Angelica was greeted there as Dr. Van Dusen by her staff of two human vets. Upon removing the old bandage, she saw that Fluffy's wounds were healing well. She dried them thoroughly, applied an herbal ointment she had made up, and re-bandaged them. While she was there, Fluffy got her feline immunization shots, which included a non-toxic flea repellent that Mama Angelica had developed herself and a quick physical exam. "You should be completely healed in a few days," said Mama Angelica. "Now let's join the others in freshman orientation."

Freshman orientation was taking place in the Great Hall. Formerly a ballroom, this vast chamber served as a combination meeting hall and gym. Sometimes basketball hoops were set up and there would be telekinetic basketball games, often between the dogs and the cats, a long-standing rivalry. This was also where Bernard held his telekinetic muscle-building classes, a required course for all students, where they would build their telekinetic powers by working with weights.

But now the entire freshman class of 2135 was gathered to hear Bernard's address. There was Fluffy's group plus about twenty more, mostly dogs and cats, but a few mice and pigs. So that they could see and be seen, and also to avoid being stepped on, the mice had a raised platform built especially for them. They also had their own entrance, a small hole from the outside of the building that led to a ramp that led to the platform.

"Welcome to all of you!" said Bernard. "I know it could not have been easy for any of you to find your way here, and I applaud your determination. Here at Animal U, we hold classes year-round. The summer semester will be starting on Wednesday, in four days. We offer instruction on all levels of learning. If you were never taught the basics of reading and writing, you can join our kindergarten group, where you will be able to learn what you'll need to know to move on to more advanced subjects. There is no shame in this; many adult GABs were never taught anything by their humans and have had to fend for themselves in the world. Before signing up for classes, everyone will be given an aptitude test. This will determine which classes you will be eligible for. Within those constraints, we invite everyone to sign up for as many or as few classes as each of you feels he or she can take on. We encourage you to pursue your areas of interest, but also to stretch your comfort zones, and study subjects that challenge your natural abilities. The one course that is required for everyone is the one taught by me (a few titters). It is called Special Powers and includes enhanced telepathy and telekinesis. The telekinesis classes are for both strength and dexterity. By the time you graduate, you will be able to lift a small car, and also tie a small bow with your mind."

He then introduced Caramel, a beautiful calico cat, the school registrar. "Caramel will be administering the aptitude test and will give each of you your own little tablet, which you are to carry with you to all classes. You can use your tablets to sign up for classes from the list provided on the school intranet, a proprietary database accessible only to students and staff. You should also use your tablets as notebooks for all subjects, to take and organize your notes, and also to access books. The school intranet contains a library of thousands of books, including all required and suggested reading for courses, and many more as well. For classes taught by non-telepathic human professors, you can use the speaker on your tablet to give you an audible voice, just like on a full-size computer. Now, are there any questions?"

Since they did not have hands to raise, the animals had a telepathic symbol they sent out, a Q, to indicate they had a question. Fluffy sent out a Q and Bernard called on her.

"Excuse me, sir," she spoke more formally to Bernard than she would have in private. "Where do these tablets come from?"

"We build them in our computer science building," said Bernard.

"But where do the parts come from?"

Bernard smiled. "A good question, Fluffy. Once a month, a cargo helicopter loaded with things we need from the outside world lands here at Animal U. All I can tell you is that there is a network of humans who help us. It's all funded by Dr. Van Dusen's family foundation."

There were several other questions, but the most provocative came, oddly enough, from Jack: "Do we get to graduate?"

"Someday, Jack, we hope to be recognized by the human world as a legitimate institution and have a four-year syllabus and a graduation ceremony and a diploma that means something in the world. For now, however, we are strictly underground, and the answer to your question is 'no.' Right now, the world is a dangerous place for all of us, so Animal U is a safe haven as well as a seat of learning. The good news is, you can stay here and learn for as long as you like. You will never be asked to leave, and you will always be fed and nurtured. There have been a few—a very few—students who have chosen to leave and go back into the world. If that is your choice, no one will stop you. But the way the world is now, what is there to go back to?"

There were murmurs of agreement. Then, since there were no more questions, the meeting was adjourned.

Caramel gave out all the tablets and asked everyone to take the aptitude test. This took about an hour. The tablets came in two sizes: regular for dogs, cats, and pigs, and tiny for mice. They were also given little backpacks that had a pouch just the right size to hold their tablet and maybe some pencils or pens. It was ingeniously designed to sit on the student's back like a saddle, with a harness for the front legs and an adjustable cinch that tightened under the chest. The strap fastened with Velcro, so, with a little practice, all of them quickly learned to don and remove their backpacks. After taking the test, each animal was given a list of classes for which they qualified. With all the homeschooling Fluffy had gotten, she qualified for almost every class. Jack had to sign up for kindergarten, but Fluffy was sure his native intelligence would get him up to speed in no time.

Now all the freshmen who had arrived before Fluffy and her party dispersed and went to their various residences, leaving Fluffy, Jack, Tigger, Stella, Leroy, and Sally.

Mamma Angelica and Bernard stayed with them.

"Would you like to take a tour of the campus?" said Bernard.

"Oh yes, please!"

Mama Angelica ushered them to a little electric golf cart that had a canvas roof and bade them hop in. She got in the driver's seat, and they were off.

First, they were shown to their residences. There were several dorms: two larger dorms for cats, four smaller dorms for dogs, one for smaller pigs, a large pen, partially shaded by a tin roof, and an enclosed dorm for cold weather for the larger pigs, and a tiny village dubbed Mousetown which had a labyrinth of hollowed-out mounds made of red clay with entrance holes where the mice loved to burrow. There were also multi-chamber residences for families, where animals who had offspring and chose to be monogamous could live with their spouse and children. This behavior was encouraged at Animal U, but not mandatory.

Then there was the nursery, which adjoined the kindergarten. It too was divided by species. Here, nursing mothers cared for their newborns until they were ready to be weaned. In the kindergarten, all species were taught together and learned at an early age to suppress their aggressive instincts toward each other. Animal U's most treasured asset was its baby GABs. In this environment, they would grow up even smarter and more powerful than they would have in the outside world and, of course, exponentially smarter than their parents.

All the buildings had solar panels on the roofs, with several larger panels out beyond the gardens. The entire campus was powered by a single Epsilon storage battery—the same kind that Lucien Epps had changed the world with generations ago.

The cat and dog dorms were long, narrow cabins, no more than eight feet high. The cats all slept in plastic laundry baskets with soft blankets folded inside. Fluffy and Sally's baskets were in Cat Dorm II. The rows of baskets were anchored in place. The lower bunks were on the floor, and the uppers were on a wide shelf about three feet off the ground. The bunks lined both sides of the cabin. In the center of the room were two rows of food and water bowls, one set for each resident. There were heavy wooden boards nailed to the floor with little hollows carved in them where each bowl sat securely. Every day, twice a day, staff members would come around with packets of food. Each packet had an animal's name on it, as did each bowl. Each animal's food packet had the food blend that Mama Angelica had prescribed for that animal. The dorm had one full-size door for the staff, a cat door at each end, and windows that slid open and closed for air in the summer and warmth in the winter. There was an electric heater for when it got cold.

Cat Dorm I was for male cats, and that was where Tigger and Jack bunked. It was a challenge to keep the male cats from fighting over silly territorial disputes or spraying to mark their territory, but Bernard and Mama Angelica were very strict about maintaining discipline, and most of the animals respected them too much to disobey. Animal U was about more than education, it was about evolution, and that included discarding instincts that had outlived their usefulness (a lesson humans had yet to learn). Stella bunked in Dog Dorm III, which was for smaller females and Leroy in Dog Dorm IV, which was for smaller males. Because of the wide disparity in dog sizes, there had to be separate sleeping pallets for large and small dogs.

As they tooled around the campus, which was about a mile-and-a-half square, Mama Angelica or Bernard would point out various structures: The science lab, the computer science building, and the two buildings where the maintenance and kitchen crews lived. "Our six maintenance people are very talented and skilled at gardening, building and fixing things," said Mama Angelica, "And we have three food service people, who cook for the human staff and also help me prepare the animals' food. They all used to live as rips in a ripcom, but they escaped. Now they live and work here all year round for a nominal salary, but are provided with food and a home. Several of them have wives, husbands, and kids, and we provide apartments for the families in that building," she said pointing to the larger building on the left.

"What are those little houses?" asked Fluffy, indicating about ten small wooden structures that dotted the campus.

"Those are outhouses," said Mama Angelica. "We're very proud of our waste management system. There is a hole in the floor of each of those little houses. That's where all animals go to the bathroom. The waste goes into a small pool of water, just like a toilet bowl, and it is then flushed into underground pipes that take it to a large underground septic tank. In that tank are millions of bacteria that consume the waste, leaving only water, which is then filtered and used to irrigate our gardens. We grow corn and carrots that the pigs and mice like to eat, soy for the animal food, and many other vegetables for the people." Then she pointed to a large barn-like shed. "That's where all the animal food is made. We have a variety of different formulae for dogs, cats, and mice, depending upon each animal's age and nutrition needs. It's all made from vegetables and certain enzymes we developed here."

"No meat?" said Tigger.

"That's right. We don't eat anything made from dead animals. That doesn't seem right, does it?" said Mama Angelica.

"But it's our natural diet," said Stella.

"When you taste the food here, you won't miss your old meat, Stella," said Bernard.

"Do Coyotes or Bears ever come here?" asked Fluffy.

"We have a razor wire fence along the outer perimeters of our campus to keep predators out. So far, none have gotten in. The fences are clearly marked with warning signs, so none of our students get hurt," said Bernard.

"What about owls and hawks?" asked Jack.

"Owls only hunt at night, so we keep the campus well-lit until it's time for everyone to retire. So far, we haven't lost any students to predatory birds," said Bernard.

"Where do they teach English and math and history?" asked Fluffy.

"In the main house, there are twenty classrooms where all those subjects and more are taught. On your tablets you'll find a map of the campus and room numbers for all the classrooms and a list of the room numbers for each subject and instructor," said Bernard.

"And what's that building?" asked Fluffy, looking at a cute wooden cottage.

"That's the grooming salon," said Mama Angelica. "We have two professional groomers on duty there every day."

"Oh, I need to go there!" said Fluffy. Her fluffy coat had taken quite a beating during her journey.

"Yes you do, Fluffy," said Mama Angelica, "and you will, once those bandages come off."

Groomers! What a wonderful place, she thought.

The next day—Sunday—Fluffy, using her new tablet, signed up for a full load of classes. Her first choice was obvious: English Lit. It was taught by an elderly cocker spaniel named Miss Dora. She also signed up for world history, basic math, and philosophy, which was taught by a pugnacious pig named Pythagoras, a massive, feisty character with quite a reputation around campus. Fluffy had read some online screeds by Pythagoras advocating a violent revolution by GABs and calling pork-eating humans "...monsters with the blood of innocents dripping from their carnivorous maws," and she couldn't resist getting to know this character in person. Of course, she had to sign up for Bernard's Special Powers class, which met three times a week. Lastly, she signed up for Genetic Theory: The History of GAB. She had done some reading on the subject and wanted to know more about how her kind had come about. This was taught by a human, Dr. Gina Ditirro, once a noted geneticist at Harvard. She had been involved with some of the last GAB experiments.

There was one other human professor at Animal U: Dr. Paul Messner, an astrophysicist who had taught at MIT long ago. Fluffy was very curious about astrophysics, the origin and future of the universe, but she had not taken enough math and science to sign up for Dr. Messner's class. She was just as curious about the man as the subject. He was reportedly the first teacher at Animal U, and Fluffy had heard an interesting story around campus about how he and his GAB German Shepherd, Rex, had gotten lost in the woods many years ago, and Mama Angelica had found them. It was rumored that Messner and Mama Angelica had some kind of romance, but there was no indication of that now. Anyway, Messner had stayed around for some reason. Rex mated with Mama Angelica's Golden Retriever, Daisy, also GAB, and the puppies were amazingly smart. That's when they decided to start Animal U, and Dr. Messner and Rex had never left. Rex and Daisy's descendants were still attending classes at Animal U.

On Monday, the bandages came off Fluffy's tail, and she went straight to the groomers. Jack went with her—he needed it more than Fluffy, having actually never been groomed at all. There were two groomers, Jill and Bob. They washed them, meticulously combed the knots out of their fur, and blew it dry. Then they got a nice brushing. Fluffy felt great to be back to her clean and fluffy self, and Jack had never looked better.

And not a moment too soon, for that night was a big party for all the incoming freshmen in the Great Hall. All the adult students and faculty would attend, and Fluffy was anxious to meet as many of them as possible.

When Jack and Fluffy entered, the party was already in full swing. Dance music emanated from a giant speaker system. At the turntable was DJ Dawg, a young beagle who deftly manipulated vinyl records on two turntables and a computer to create an ongoing groove that was dominated by thumping bass and drums. These twenty-first-century artifacts, along with the skills to use them, had been handed down to Dawg by his father, who had also been DJ Dawg. His father and his father before him had all been DJ Dawgs. It was the family trade, you might say. Many of the animals were doing the four-legged strut, a dance invented at Animal U. Two French poodles were showing off their moves on hind legs, just like circus dogs. The mice danced on their elevated platform.

There were exotic snacks and pure spring water for the animals, and the people ate hors-d'oeuvres and drank euphorium champagne.

After the DJ set, it was time for the drum circle. Three of the men in the maintenance crew were descended from the Tuareg people, a nomadic tribe of North Africa, and they brought with them a tradition of hand drumming. The animals clamored for them to perform at every opportunity. Each guy had a drum of a different size and timbre: there was a giant bass drum, a mid-range drum, and a high drum. There was something about the sound of the human hand on the drumhead (which was made from the skin of an animal) that mesmerized the animals. Hands were something they didn't have, so this was a thing only humans could do. The drummers sat in a triangle in the center of the hall, and the animals formed a circle around them. They started with a slow, hypnotic, mid-tempo rhythm, with the deep bass drum starting every bar with a resounding "boom" on the downbeat. The animals swayed to the rhythm and began to slowly circle the drummers to the beat. Leading the circle dance was a group of graceful cats who performed a slinky cat dance, moving, with two steps forward and one step back, in perfect unison. Fluffy watched in utter fascination, desperately wanting to join in the dance, but not quite sure how to do it.

Then something very strange happened. Sally, the young female tabby who had been rescued by Bernard along with Jack and the others, suddenly exited the hall, moving fast and looking distressed. As she passed, Fluffy picked up an odd scent, new but somehow familiar. About half the male cats in the room, Jack and Tigger included, followed her out onto the grassy quad in the center of the campus. Curious, Fluffy followed. Sally was in the middle of the quad, emitting unearthly moaning sounds, which she, herself, plainly did not understand.

Meanwhile, the males circled, and the largest, a big tom named Rocky, moved in on Sally from behind. Jack rushed forward, hissing and challenging Rocky. Then a squad of six senior classmen, three cats and three dogs, rushed out of the hall. The spokesman for this group was a sleek black cat named Luna. "Back off, you two," she said to Rocky and Jack.

"What's happening to me?" said Sally.

"Don't worry, sweetie. You're in heat," said Luna. "It's a perfectly natural thing, but we have rules about this here."

"What d'ya mean, rules?" said Jack.

"Yeah, what d'ya mean?" echoed Rocky.

"We want to have as many GAB babies as we can at Animal U, but we can't allow random mating, and we can't allow a female to be taken by multiple males. This is another case of overcoming our base instincts so that we can evolve. Here's how it works: She gets to choose the father of her babies. Often it helps the female decide if a suitor makes a proposal of marriage. He has to swear in front of us—the civilian referees—eternal faithfulness to the female and that he will stay with her and help raise her babies. Are any of you willing to make that commitment?" she asked, scanning the male suitors.

"I am," said Jack. "Sally, I've loved you from the first moment we met. I'll stay with you."

Sally looked at Jack, then at the far bigger and stronger Rocky. "I've always loved you too, Jack. I would have picked you even if you hadn't said anything."

"Okay, it's decided then," said Luna. "The rest of you boys, back to the dance. Sally and Jack, have fun!" She sent them a winking smiley face.

All the male cats filed back into the dance. Jack and Sally slipped away into the shadows.

Fluffy, who had been observing from afar, was very impressed with the idea of civilian referees. *Such a civilized way to resolve conflicts*, she thought. She approached Luna. "What makes you a civilian referee?" she asked.

"There's only two qualifications: You have to be spayed or neutered, and you have to volunteer. Do you want to volunteer?"

"I think so, but I don't know if I've been spayed," said Fluffy.

"You have," said Luna. "I can tell. But have Dr. Van Dusen check you out and get a confirmation letter from her, and then come see me. Now, let's get back to the party."

Fluffy looked around for Jack, but he and Sally had already disappeared. *Wow, I guess I'm going to be an aunt.*

The next day was Tuesday. Fluffy asked to speak with Mama Angelica in her office. "Mama Angelica, have I been spayed?"

"You're a five-year-old cat. Have you ever come into heat?"

"Not that I know of."

"You'd know if you had. Yes, Fluffy, you have been spayed."

"Good," said Fluffy. "It looks very messy and complicated to mate, and have to have babies and all that."

"It's not for everyone, but for many, it's very fulfilling," said Mama Angelica.

"I'm going to volunteer as a civilian referee," said Fluffy.

"I think you'll make a splendid civilian referee, Fluffy." She took Fluffy's tablet and typed a letter confirming her status. "Just show this to Luna," she said.

"Thank you, Mama Angelica." And off she went to find Luna and volunteer. On the way, she passed the family dwellings for cats and saw

Jack and Sally. They were setting up housekeeping in a roomy space. "Hi," said Fluffy. "I'm very happy for you both. I can't wait to see those kittens."

"Thanks, Fluffy," said Jack. "We're very happy. And none of this would have happened if not for you. I owe you everything."

"In a way, I owe my new life to you, Jack," said Fluffy. "I wouldn't have left home if you hadn't called out to me." They all rubbed up against each other, and Fluffy moved on. She found Luna in her bunk in Cat Dorm II and signed up to be a Civilian Referee.

"It's not very hard," said Luna. "Just use your common sense. Sometimes we also have to intervene in fights. When there are six or seven of us standing there watching, that alone is usually enough to defuse any argument. If there is a serious enough issue, two students can take their dispute before the Student Council and have it resolved by them."

"How do you get on the Student Council?" asked Fluffy.

"There are elections once a year, but you have to be at least a sophomore to run," said Luna.

The next day was Wednesday, the first day of classes, and Fluffy had three classes on her schedule: English Lit, Special Powers, and Basic Math. She felt good about the first two, but math was not a strong subject for her, and she felt a little trepidation about it.

In English Lit, Miss Dora took an immediate shine to Fluffy. It turned out that Fluffy had already read more than half the books on the reading list—works by Jane Austin, the Brontë sisters, Oscar Wilde, Charles Dickens, Shakespeare, F. Scott Fitzgerald, Thomas Hardy, Ernest Hemingway, Kurt Vonnegut, John Fowles, Dan Brown, S.J. Watson, Alice Sebold—and this impressed Miss Dora tremendously.

In Special Powers, Bernard showed the freshmen how to exercise their powers by lifting weights telekinetically and by honing in on the telepathic messages from one animal across the entire campus, isolating that one voice from all of the cross-chatter going on all around. She practiced sending and receiving visual images as well. And then Bernard showed them something truly remarkable: his Telepathy Amplifier. This consisted of a headset that fit over the crown of an animal's head like a cap, but it was fitted with tiny electrodes that tapped into the telepathy centers of the brain. It plugged into an electronic device with a rotating dish on top that could be aimed in any direction.

"Using this device," Bernard said, "one can locate one or a group of telepathic beings anywhere in the world and have a two-way conversation with them. I used this to hone in on you, Fluffy, and send you those 'advertisements' for Animal U."

"Well, they certainly worked," said Fluffy. "But how did it find me?"

"The Amplifier has a Scan setting. It can scan a geographical radius of up to 1,000 miles for GABs with exceptional telepathic powers. When it finds one, we send out the message. The messages we sent to you, we also sent to hundreds of other animals. They may not all figure out the clues, and they won't all find their way here, but as you know, we always have someone waiting in the cabin by the falls to receive new arrivals."

Then Fluffy asked, "Have you spoken with GABs in other countries?"

"I have. There are several universities very much like ours in Europe, Africa, and Asia, and I have communicated with them all. I've shared the blueprint for this machine with them, so we can establish a worldwide telepathic network."

The class was suitably impressed, and there was excited conversation about the possibilities of this invention, how it will unite all GABs and give them more power to fight human oppression.

After class, Fluffy went back to her dorm for lunch and a cat nap before the dreaded math. She set the alarm on her tablet, and it woke her up in a half hour.

Math was taught by a neutered male cat named Mr. Fritz. Fritz had been raised and educated in Germany by a professor of mathematics, so he spoke with a slight German accent. "Most of you have grown up doing simple calculations on your tablets or handhelds. The goal of this class is to teach you to use your brain instead of a calculator to add, subtract, multiply, and divide. Later, we will do fractions, decimal points, and percentages. First, I will show you how to add two large numbers, using an old-fashioned pencil and a piece of paper." He gave everyone a pad of lined paper and a pencil. On the chalkboard behind him, a piece of chalk wrote two five-digit numbers, one above the other, and a line below them. He drew a plus sign in between and to the left of the two numbers. "We will start with simple addition. Everyone copy what I have written on the board." Fortunately, Fluffy had learned to color with crayons and to write with pencils and pens before she learned to use a computer. Some of the others had a harder time with this, but Fluffy lifted her pencil and copied the numbers neatly without a problem.

Basic math turned out to be much less difficult for Fluffy than she had imagined. Soon, in fact, she began to think it was fun. The first day, the class learned simple addition and subtraction. Before long, they would move on to memorizing multiplication tables and long division.

As the days went by, Fluffy's brain was fairly throbbing with all the new stimuli. She made many new friends, and she was doing well in her classes. She felt that she was at last in her element. *If only my dad could be here with me; then it would truly be perfect.*

There was one cat about Fluffy's age, Pandora, who was particularly friendly. Pandora was an almost-pure-bred Blue Point Siamese. She was light gray, which gradually got a bit darker around her face, had long pointy ears, and beautiful blue eyes. Pandora was in several of Fluffy's classes and lived in the same dorm, so they often walked to and from class together. Pandora was very competitive, and sensing a worthy opponent in Fluffy, she was constantly challenging Fluffy in class: who knew more facts, who could get the higher marks on exams… Fluffy treated all this with good humor, and she consistently bested Pandora in every contest. Sometimes Pandora got visibly upset, so Fluffy started to let her win occasionally. Pandora was as bad a winner as she was a loser, chuckling derisively every time she got the best of Fluffy. One day in Bernard's telekinesis muscle-building class, the competition got a bit intense, with Fluffy and Pandora lifting ever-heavier weights. This time Fluffy did not let Pandora win, and Pandora stormed out of the class. Fluffy went after her and caught up with her near their dorm.

"Don't be upset, Pandora. I thought this was all in good fun. We're still friends, right?"

"Yes, we're still friends," said Pandora. But there was something in the way she said it that made Fluffy uneasy.

After that, their relationship got cooler, and Fluffy stopped comparing scores with Pandora.

CHAPTER TWELVE — SAVING DAVE

Tuesday morning, Riordan opened his eyes and a vision of loveliness slowly came into focus. It was the smiling face of Indira beside him. *So it wasn't a dream; it really happened.*

They got up, had breakfast, and took the supertube to Kingston. Riordan donned his new/old broad-brimmed fedora and trench coat and told Indira, "We gotta case the joint, baby." So they made their way to the massive 200-story Epsilon complex.

As expected, there was a security system in place that made everybody pass through a portal which was a combined X-ray and metal detector. Once inside the lobby, they followed the signs to the Convention Center. This was a separate building, accessed through a long corridor. Inside the vast hall, a crew of robots and people were in the process of setting up for the Robotics Conference. There was a high stage at one end of the room, big enough to stage a Broadway musical. In front of that was a dais with a speaker's podium. On the floor, the crew was setting up row upon row of folding chairs—about 2,000 of them. There were two tiers of balcony seating on three sides of the room. Around the outer perimeter of the wooden floor, a dirt track about six feet wide had been installed.

"I'll bet that's for Penelope," Indira said, and they shared another chuckle.

They walked back to the lobby of the Epsilon Tower and took the elevator to Roof Parking. There was a small lobby and a doorway with a small glass window marked HELIPAD. Inside it was a stairwell, with a few steps leading up to the glass doors that opened onto the roof helipad and 201 flights of metal steps going down to the ground floor. They surveyed the layout and Riordan made a few notes, then they ascended onto the roof. A security guard emerged from a kiosk. "May I see your parking pass, folks?"

"Err, we just came up to look at the view," said Riordan.

"I'm sorry. You need a parking pass to be up here."

Indira and Riordan scoped the helipad. There were five robocopters parked there. "Aww," said Indira, hamming it up. "Gosh, I bet you can see the whole city from up here."

"Okay, thanks anyway," said Riordan, and they went back down. They descended in the elevator that made their stomachs rise into their chests.

"I hope we can identify Epps's robocopter," said Indira. "How are we gonna get past that guard?"

"I have an idea," said Riordan. "Know any place where we can buy fireworks?"

"No, but I bet Bobby does."

Bobby told his boss, Dr. Barenholtz, that he had invited Indira and her friend, Professor Kute, an English professor from Berkeley, to join the MIT Robotics Team for the conference. Like everyone at MIT, Barenholtz had a soft spot for Indira, so he gave his permission. Thursday morning, Riordan and Indira showed up at the Robotics lab in their Team MIT coveralls and name tags. Riordan slipped the gun and a cherry bomb to Bobby, who inserted them into their designated hiding place, and they loaded Penelope into the truck. They had even enlisted a little girl, about nine, to ride her around the track. Little Amelia Reynolds was an experienced equestrian, and she was all decked out in her traditional English riding costume.

At the Epsilon Building, the truck backed up to the loading dock, and the team wheeled Penelope onto the dock, where she passed through the X-ray/metal detector. As expected, she sent the metal detector into paroxysms of beeping, but then, so did all the robots being loaded in that day, since their skeletons were all made of titanium/aluminum alloy. But she passed the true test—the X-ray—with flying colors, thanks to her lead-lined rump.

Penelope was stationed onstage, behind the closed curtains, until her big moment arrived. Riordan appointed himself her personal guardian and, when no one was around, he reached under her tail and grabbed the contraband from her anal cavity.

"Excuse *me*," a voice said from behind. Riordan was caught with his hand up the horse's bum. He turned abruptly to see Mrs. Marsden, the matronly lady who was the event coordinator. *She's caught me* in flagrante dilecto!

"Oh, just untangling some knots in her tail," said the professor, meticulously separating the strands.

"Oh," said Mrs. Marsden. "It looked like something else." She tittered and walked on. Riordan quickly stashed the gun and cherry bomb in the deep pockets of his coveralls and went to find Indira. She was sitting with little Amelia, while Bobby and Dr. Barenholtz tested Penelope's remote.

Riordan pulled Indira aside. "How long does this thing go on?" he whispered. "How should I know? Epps is giving the keynote speech, so we can't miss that."

"We must get to Epps's robocopter before he does, so that means we have to disappear before he's done speaking."

"But I'm sure he'll stick around to see his new toys."

"We can't chance it. During his speech, I'll tell Barenholtz you've fallen ill, and I have to get you home at once."

"Okay. Shall I faint?"

"You're a born thespian, but let's not overdo it," said Riordan. "Have a seat and I'll give you your cue."

Out front, the seats had all filled with robotics enthusiasts:

retailers, wholesalers, private buyers, and journalists. The lights went down and a spotlight illuminated the speaker's podium. Popular standup comedian Jasper Figgus, a slight, manic black guy with a flattop haircut, stepped up to the microphone to enthusiastic applause.

"Hey! Thank you, thank you so much. Good evening ladies and mechanisms." Modest laughter "How many of you like robots?" Every hand goes up, rousing applause. "How many of you *are* robots?" Laughter, a couple of people raise their hands. Jasper points to one. "Oh, out of the closet!" Laughter. "No, but seriously, I love robots. They are the most efficient, competent workers... Of course, there is the occasional glitch. The other day I saw a beautiful pair of shoes in a store window. That's right, a *real store*! I hate buying shoes online because I have these odd-shaped feet." He traces a jagged asymmetrical shape in the air. Laughter and applause. "So, I go in and I ask the salesbot, 'can I see a pair of those in size ten medium?' The guy goes away and comes back with a pair of ladies pumps—" A few titters. "Red, with stiletto heels. Lady's size six." Laughter. "So, I go, 'No, *these*,' and I point again to the men's shoes in the window. So, he goes away and comes back with a pair of lady's pink fuzzy slippers." More laughter. "So, I'm, like, 'oh man, dis bot done blew a fuse.'" Big laugh. "So, I go to the manager, pull him aside, and I say 'hey man, there's something wrong with your salesbot there. The manager looks at the guy and says 'He's not a bot. He's the token human!'" Loud laughter and applause. "And speaking of artificial intelligence, I was having dinner with my wife the other night—" Loud laughter. "Okay, scratch intelligence." More laughter. Jasper pauses. "Now, as we all know, Epsilon makes the best robots money can buy." Applause. "In fact, the *only* robots money can buy." Laughter. "And tonight, it is my great pleasure and a true honor to introduce to you my idol, the president and CEO of Epsilon Industries, a man who, not only needs no introduction but probably wishes he hadn't had this one, Mr. Jeremiah Epps!" Thunderous applause, as Epps ascends the podium and shakes hands with Jasper.

"Jasper Figgus, ladies, and gentlemen!" Epps gives Jasper a pat on the back as he leaves the podium. "Over a century ago, my great, great grandfather started the robotics program at Epsilon. We've come a long way since then…"

Backstage, Riordan says to Indira, "Okay, now's the time." Indira slumps down in her chair, takes out a handkerchief and starts mopping her brow. Riordan goes over and whispers something to Barenholtz. Barenholtz nods.

"Let's go." Riordan helps Indira to her feet. He surreptitiously transfers the gun and the cherry bomb to his trench coat pocket and they both shed their coveralls. They exit through the auditorium, getting a good look at Epps on their way out. In the elevator, they both actually need the handkerchief, as they are both now sweating profusely.

On the top floor, Riordan peers through the small glass window in the door that leads to the stairwell and the roof. He motions her to stay there, goes into the stairwell, and checks outside. The roof and helipad are illuminated with bright spotlights. The night security guard is in his kiosk.

Riordan returns to the lobby. "Here goes…" He lights the fuse on the cherry bomb, opens the stairwell door, and tosses it down the stairwell. Three seconds go by, then a loud BOOM echoes through the stairwell. The guard runs in from his post and starts down the stairs, gun drawn. As soon as he is down one flight, Indira and Riordan silently enter the stairwell, ascend the few steps to the helipad and are out on the roof. In the center is the circular landing pad, ringed with small lights. There are six robocopters parked on the roof. "The one with the Epsilon logo has got to be his," says Indira. Riordan tries the door; it's not locked. They tilt the front seat forward and climb into the back seat. There's plenty of room on the floor to crouch down when Epps gets in. Riordan takes out the gun. "How do you use this thing?"

"Here, give it to me," says Indira. It's an old 9 mm Walther automatic. She expertly takes off the safety and cocks it, putting one round in the chamber.

"Great," says Riordan. "You're in charge of the firearms… Say, we could be waiting here a long time. What should we do?" She kisses him, and they start making out.

"Okay, let's not get carried away," he says. "We don't want to be caught 'napping.'" He looks out the copter window. "I wish we could've seen Penelope do her stuff."

"Yeah, I'm sure Bobby wishes we could've seen it too. Hey, is this him?" They peer out of the window, and, sure enough, here comes Epps.

"Get down!" whispers Indira.

"I am down!"

"Shhhh!"

The pilot's side door of the copter opens and Epps climbs into his seat. He pushes some presets, and the copter takes off.

During the fifteen-minute flight, Riordan and Indira barely dare to breathe. She clutches onto his arm so hard he almost cries out, but instead gently loosens her grip. At last, Epps's copter sets itself down on his rooftop helipad, just as it has every evening for years. Epps exits the pilot side door, walks around to the passenger side, and starts toward the door that leads to the stairs.

"Now!" whispers Indira, and they push the front seat forward and both charge through the narrow passenger side door simultaneously, getting jammed together in the doorway. Epps turns to see Riordan trip and hit the ground as Indira stumbles out of the copter brandishing the gun.

"Hold it right there, Mr. Epps!" says Indira.

"Yeah, hold it right there," says Riordan lamely.

Epps laughs. "What is this, a holdup by Laurel and Hardy? Did Figgus send you guys as a practical joke?"

By this time Riordan has brushed himself off and regained his composure, if not his dignity.

"We've come for Dr. Handler," says Indira. She looks serious enough to wipe the smile off Epps's face.

He indicates the gun. "Is that thing real?"

"It's very real, and we won't hesitate to use it," says Riordan. "You see, we know the world is coming to an end, so we have nothing to lose. Now put your hands up." Epps puts his hands up, still not really taking this seriously.

"Frisk him," says Indira.

Riordan points to himself with a question mark on his face and silently mouths the word "Me?" She gestures with the gun for him to go ahead and frisk Epps. Riordan shrugs and does his best to imitate the old-time cops frisking a guy.

Epps laughs again. "Hey, cut it out, that tickles." Then he addresses Indira. "I'll bet you don't even know which end of that gun shoots the bullets." She fires a shot and misses his foot by a centimeter. He recoils, regards her with new respect. So does Riordan.

At the sound of the shot, Hobson and two other security guys come charging out onto the roof, guns drawn. Indira moves closer to Epps, turns him around, puts the gun to his back.

"Tell them to drop their guns."

"Do as she says, Hobson." The security guys drop their guns. Riordan scrambles to pick them up. He pats them all down to see if they have any more, comes up with a pair of handcuffs.

"Hey, these might come in handy," he says and handcuffs Epps's hands behind his back.

"Get the key," says Indira.

"Key," says Riordan. The second security guy tosses him the handcuff key. "Now, take us to Dr. Handler. Everybody walk nice and slow."

Hobson leads the way, followed by the two security guards. Riordan, with one of the confiscated guns trained on the guy in front of him, is followed by Epps. Bringing up the rear is Indira with a gun in his back. They descend the spiral wrought iron staircase that leads to the room Epps calls his study.

Unlike the living room, the study is more masculine: brown wood paneling, floor-to-ceiling bookshelves, fireplace, a fully-stocked bar, a desk, computer, and a collection of antique works of art that is unrivaled anywhere in the world: Original Matisses, Van Goghs,

Picassos, Miros.

"Percy, you wait here with the Pinkertons. Epps, take me to Dave," says Indira. Minutes later Indira and Epps return with Dr. Handler.

"Dave!" Riordan hasn't seen his old college buddy in thirty years.

"Jimmy?"

"It's Percy at the moment, but never mind."

"What are you doing here?"

"We've come to spring you, as we say in the criminal underworld."

"Dave," Indira cuts in, "we need your help." Then, to Epps and his security guys: "Okay, here's what's going to happen: Dave, Percy and me, and Mr. E here are going to get back on that robocopter. We are going to fly outta here. Anybody tries to stop us or follow us, Epps gets it first."

"Wait," says Handler. "My computer. They've got it locked up somewhere."

"Where is it?" says Indira.

"It's locked in a storage room downstairs," says Hobson.

"Go get it. Percy, you go with him."

Riordan accompanies Hobson out of the room. They return a few minutes later with a small leather carrying case. Riordan gives it to Handler, then he leads the way up the stairs, followed by Handler. Indira, goes up backward, using Epps as a shield and keeping her gun on the security guys, who stay in the study. Once on the roof, they all pile into the robocopter. Riordan sits in the "pilot's" seat, with Epps next to him in front. Indira shows Riordan how to punch in the coordinates for West Kill Falls, and they take off.

The flight was brief, but Riordan couldn't resist asking Handler, "David, is there nothing we can do to stop this asteroid? Couldn't we explode a nuclear bomb to knock it off its course?"

It was Epps that answered. "Where did you say you were a professor?"

"I didn't."

"Well, professor, if you knew anything about recent history, you would know that we don't have nukes anymore. All weapons of mass destruction and the means to deliver them were destroyed after the Treaty of 2105 when the corporations consolidated power."

"But surely we could build one…"

"No," said Handler. "There's not enough time. We would have to start from raw uranium; it would take too long to get enough and to enrich it to weapons grade. We don't have centrifuges. And we don't have any missiles to launch it."

"We're over the falls," said Indira. "Turn on the searchlight."

Riordan found the switch that turned on the searchlight and trained it on the terrain below. They could see the stream and the falls, and a road about 100 feet away. There was a van parked near the footpath that led to the falls.

"That must be Art," said Riordan.

"Where are we anyway?" said Epps.

"We're in a secret place. If I told you, I'd have to kill you," said Riordan, getting a bit carried away with his new persona. "It's just a hunch, but I have a feeling we might be able to find some answers here."

The copter set itself down on the road near the car. "That you, professor?" It was Art's voice. The van door opened and Art emerged.

"Yes, Art. And I brought some friends—and an enemy."

Art was dumbstruck. "But that's…"

"Jeremiah Epps, in person," said Riordan. "And these are my friends, Indira and Dr. David Handler, the world's foremost astronomer."

Now Laura got out of the van, carrying a shoebox, and joined them. Art introduced Laura to everyone.

"What's in the box?" asked Indira.

Laura opened the shoebox and inside were Hacker and Mitzi, who was nursing six tiny mouse babies. "Say hello to Hacker, Mitzi and the family," said Laura. "Hacker's the gray one."

"Hi," said Hacker.

Riordan, Indira, Handler, and Epps were agog. "How did he do that?" said Epps.

"Hey, first things first. Aren't you gonna congratulate me? I'm a dad!"

"Congratulations," they all murmured in unison.

"The voice disc is Hacker's latest invention. I guess you could call him the Edison of rodents," said Art.

"Fantastic," said Handler.

"You think I'm smart, just wait until these little critters grow up. Of course, if you have your way, they never will, will they, Mr. Epps?"

Everyone turns to Epps. He actually looks sheepish. For the first time in his life, Jeremiah Epps is at a loss for words.

"Hacker, do you think you could contact Fluffy? I'm pretty sure she's near here," said Riordan.

"I haven't got a lot of experience at long distance telepathy, but Fluffy and I were pretty close, so maybe..."

"Well, can you try?"

"Look, could somebody please tell us what this is all about?" said Art.

"Oh, sorry, Art," said Riordan. Then he looked searchingly at Indira and Handler. *How do I tell someone the world's about to end?*

"I'll do it," said Handler. "Art, Laura, Hacker, there's an asteroid the size of New Jersey headed straight for Earth. It's traveling 18,000 miles per hour and it's twelve million, nine hundred and sixty thousand miles away. In twenty-five days it will be here, and it will destroy the Earth."

"Unless...?" said Art.

"I don't know," said Handler.

"I don't know either," said Riordan, "but I just have this feeling Fluffy and her friends at Animal U might have the answer. So, Hacker..."

Everyone turned their gaze toward the small gray mouse in the shoebox. Hacker was motionless. For a long time, there was no sound but falling water and the wind through the trees.

"She says to tell you she loves you, Doc. She congratulated me and Mitzi on our babies…"

"And…?" said everyone.

"And she's consulting her crew about letting us come to Animal U. I think the snag is, ahem, you, Mr. Epps. Wait…I'm getting something…They say Epps can come. He might learn something."

"Wonderful," said Riordan. "Now what?"

"First of all," said Hacker, "cover this shoebox with something. You're all gonna get wet, but not my babies."

"Here," said Riordan, "cover it with my raincoat." He passed his raincoat to Laura.

"Fluffy and two others are coming to escort us. It'll take about an hour," said Hacker.

"We've got to get rid of that robocopter," said Riordan. "We've got to hide it somewhere."

"Maybe we can shove it off a cliff or something," said Indira.

So, Indira flew the robocopter up the mountain until she got to a place where there was a long sheer drop beside the road. Riordan and Art followed in the van. Laura and Handler stayed behind to keep an eye on Epps, who seemed lost in thought and kept silent. Indira set the copter down by the edge of the cliff, and they pushed it over the side with the van. They watched as the small craft bounced off the rocky face and broke into a thousand pieces even before it hit bottom. "Well, they'll have a hard time finding that," said Indira. Then they drove back to the falls and waited.

At last, they heard a voice—a voice Riordan recognized. It was Fluffy. "Down here," she shouted. Her real voice projected through the voice disc still sounded remarkably like Katharine Hepburn's. The voice was coming from under the falls. Fluffy guided the group across the footbridge and down the eastern bank to the edge of the stream, then up the mossy stone "steps" that led to the cavern. One by one, they crawled through the falling water and into the low-ceilinged cave: Epps went first, so he couldn't make a break for it—they had taken off his handcuffs so he could negotiate the climb, then came Indira, then

Handler, Riordan, Art, and Laura, bearing the shoebox covered with Riordan's raincoat. Riordan embraced Fluffy. He saw the fur had been shaved off part of her tail and the remnants of the wounds. "Are you alright?"

"I'm fine," said Fluffy. "I can't believe you're here, Dad!"

"I guess we both have some tales to tell—er, no pun intended. Fluffy, this is my good friend, Indira."

Fluffy looked between her dad and Indira and sensed their love.

"I've heard so much about you, Fluffy," said Indira. "So great to finally meet you." She couldn't resist reaching out and stroking Fluffy's head.

"It's great to meet you too, Indira," said Fluffy. She couldn't help wondering if she had a rival for her dad's love.

With Fluffy were Bernard and Mama Angelica. Fluffy introduced them and Riordan introduced his party. "And this is Jeremiah Epps," Riordan said at last, with a mixture of pride at his capture and trepidation at how he would be received.

"Welcome to all of you," said Mama Angelica. "Even you, Mr. Epps." Then, to Indira: "You'll have to leave your gun here, young lady. They're neither allowed nor needed where we're going."

"I think I've got one too—in my raincoat," said Riordan. Laura got the gun out of his pocket and tossed it aside.

Fluffy asked Laura to open the box, just for a moment, so she could say hello to Hacker and Mitzi and see the babies.

"Hi, Fluffy," said Hacker. "So here we are, all together again."

"Congratulations, Hacker and Mitzi," said Fluffy. "The next generation of GAB mice is here. Now the world will truly see something—if the world survives."

Then Bernard made the stone gate open and they all entered the long tunnel. Riordan started to put the handcuffs back on Epps. "You don't need to do that," said Epps. "I won't make any trouble."

"He speaks the truth," said Mama Angelica. Riordan pocketed the handcuffs, and they set off.

CHAPTER THIRTEEN — EVE OF DESTRUCTION

"Astrologers? What do you mean astrologers?" Valerie Trump was on her handheld, trying to make sense out of Hobson's rattled ramblings.

"Maybe it's astronomers," said Hobson.

"Okay, let's take it from the top one more time: Epps was kidnapped by a pair of academic types who were there to free a certain Dr. Handler, who is an astronomer Epps was holding hostage at the house?"

"Right."

"And you say there are six more 'astrologers' being held prisoner at one of the guest houses on the property?"

"That's right."

"But why was he holding scientists captive?"

"I don't know. You know Epps. He gives orders, I take 'em. No questions."

"Yes, I know him. And what about his robocopter? Have you been able to trace it?"

"It had an automatic GP signal. We traced it to the top of West Kill Mountain in the Catskills; then we lost it."

"I want to speak to those scientists."

"Of course."

"I'll be landing on the roof in half an hour."

"Very good, Miss Trump."

Valerie Trump hung up and headed straight for her robocopter. She punched in the coordinates for the Epps estate and took off.

Including Handler, there were seven astronomers in the Western Hemisphere who had discovered the asteroid. Epps had them all rounded up and flown to his estate within an hour after his Asian counterpart, Ho Chung Tanaka, had informed Epps and Himmelmann that one of his Chinese astronomers had discovered the impending doom.

Hobson met Valerie on the Epps helipad. "We have surveillance footage of the abduction. From that camera right there," said Hobson pointing to the surveillance camera just above the door that led to the spiral staircase. He took out his handheld and showed the footage to Valerie. "Face recognition software has identified both of them." He froze on Riordan as he tumbled out of the robocopter. "This is James Riordan, wanted for animal terrorist activities. The woman is Indira Afia Fitzpatrick, Dr. Handler's assistant."

"Could this have something to do with animal terrorists?"

"I don't know."

The other six astronomers were billeted under the watchful eyes of robot guards and attack robodogs in a six-bedroom guest house not far from the main house on the Epps estate. By now it was ten o'clock at night, and three of the six had retired to their rooms. The other three: Somes from Yerkes in Wisconsin, Kandinsky from Mauna Kea in Hawaii, and Calderon from the VLT (Very Large Telescope) in Chile. Somes was reading one of the many volumes provided in the large bookcase against one wall and Kandinsky and Calderon were engaged in an intense game of chess when Valerie Trump, with Hobson in tow, entered the room.

"Gentlemen," said Hobson, "this is Valerie Trump, acting CEO of Epsilon." He introduced the three scientists to Valerie.

"But what happened to Epps?" said Somes.

"We don't know," said Valerie, filling in as few details as possible. "He's disappeared. Now, I need to know why he has kidnapped you."

"You mean, neither of you knows?" said Kandinsky. Valerie and

Hobson both shook their heads. Kandinsky began to laugh. The other two joined in.

"My god," said Calderon, "the world is about to end, and Epps and us are the only ones who know!" They all had another good laugh.

"What do you mean 'the world is about to end'?"

All the men started talking at once. "I'll tell it," said Somes. "There is an asteroid about one-eighth the mass of our moon headed straight for Earth. When it gets here, it will obliterate our planet."

Valerie was stunned into silence. She swallowed hard. "And when will it get here?"

"Twenty-five days."

She looked at the calendar on her handheld. "So, the world ends July second. Is there anything anybody can do about it?"

"Nada," said Calderon.

"And you and Epps are the only ones who know?" said Valerie.

"Well, actually," said Kandinsky, "other astronomers in other parts of the world have also disappeared. I heard it on the news. So, Epps's counterparts in the Triumvirate must also know."

"You mean, between all you geniuses, and all the other geniuses in the world, no one can figure out how to stop the world from ending?"

"That's about it," said Somes.

"I can understand why they kept it a secret," said Valerie. "But somehow I think Epps, Tanaka, and Himmelmann must have also cooked up some kind of plan." She dials up her assistant. "Ivan, this is an emergency. I need to you to get me the numbers for Tanaka and Himmelmann, then conference them and patch me in."

Valerie told Tanaka and Himmelmann of Epps's kidnapping, and that she is taking the reins of Epsilon, at least temporarily. She told them she knows about the asteroid and they fill her in on the evacuation plan. "So you've each chosen 10,000 elite to leave the planet with you and now we need to choose 10,000 from the Western Hemisphere, correct? ...And what is the date of departure? ...June thirtieth. We'll be ready." She hung up and got Ivan on the phone again. "Ivan, I want you to call all members of the top management team...

Yes, right now... I don't care what time it is... So wake them up! Tell them I'm convening an emergency meeting in thirty minutes in the main conference room. It's mandatory!" Then she turned to Hobson and the astronomers. "Thank you, gentlemen, your cooperation is greatly appreciated. There is, in fact, a plan in place to evacuate as many people as possible to another planet. We leave for Moonbase June twenty-ninth. Of course, you and your families will all be included in the evacuation."

"Miss Trump, what about Mr. Epps?" said Hobson.

"What about him?"

"Shouldn't we send out a search party?"

"To hell with him," said Valerie. "He's probably being beaten and tortured by a bunch of animal terrorists right now, and as far as I'm concerned, they can have him!" Stone-faced, she gave them a stiff, cursory nod, turned on her heel, and headed for her robocopter.

When the stone curtains parted and Riordan, Indira, and the others exited the tunnel, they beheld the Animal U campus illuminated by hundreds of amber-tinted street lamps. "How can you have kept all this a secret from the Triumvirate?" asked Riordan.

"It hasn't been easy," said Mama Angelica. "Having a lot of financial resources helps. We blocked off the road that led here, jack-hammered it into dust, and let nature do the rest. We hacked into all map apps and deleted this location. We made it look like unpopulated wilderness. For fifteen years we've managed to keep it a secret from the Triumvirate and the D.I.S. Of course, that will all be over now. I certainly hope your visit is worth it."

As they approached the main house, Fluffy spoke up: "Bernard, I have an idea. Perhaps if all of us put our heads together—literally—we can make that asteroid miss us. Do you think we could use the principles of your Telepathy Amplifier to build a Telekinesis Amplifier? Maybe we can harness the telekinetic powers of all of us and amplify them to change the course of that thing."

"That thought crossed my mind too, Fluffy. It's certainly worth discussing," said Bernard. "Suppose we all go inside and 'put our heads together'?"

Inside the main house, they were greeted by Dr. Paul Messner, the astrophysicist. When Fluffy apprised her of the asteroid situation, Mama Angelica had immediately asked Dr. Messner to join the meeting. "Everyone, this is Dr. Paul Messner. He's one of our professors, an astrophysicist."

"Dr, Messner! Do you remember me? You were teaching at MIT when I first started there as an associate professor. David Handler?"

Dr. Messner was old, and it took him a minute to process this strange reunion. "Of course, David Handler, the astronomer!" They shook hands and embraced warmly.

Mama Angelica led them into the large lecture room on the ground floor, and they convened around a long table. The human contingent consisted of David Handler, Indira, Riordan, Art, Laura, Mama Angelica (introduced as Dr. Van Dusen), Epps, and Dr. Messner. The animal contingent consisted of Fluffy, Bernard, and Hacker. Art carefully lifted Hacker out of the shoebox and set him on the table. Mitzi and her brood stayed inside. Bernard sat on one of the chairs and Fluffy jumped up onto the table with Hacker. Dave took his big computer (about the size of a glossy magazine) out of its case, turned it on and keyed in the code that linked it to the Galileo telescope. They pulled down the big screen and saw what was on Dave's computer screen. Dave aimed the telescope in the direction of the asteroid, magnified, focused and pointed his cursor arrow at the asteroid. "It doesn't look like much from here, but when I do this..." He magnified it 100 times "...you can really see what we're dealing with." What they saw was a huge asymmetrical rock with ominous sharp angles protruding on all sides, tumbling end over end through space, coming at them at a terrifying speed.

Bernard, who wore his tablet in his backpack, spoke aloud for the first time. "Fluffy made a suggestion that sounds like it might work. If we can build a device that can harness and project the telekinetic powers of many GABs, aim it at the asteroid, and make it change its course, we might be able to save the Earth."

"The power of some of these animals is unbelievable," said Dr. Messner. "Why, Bernard here can lift more than twenty tons straight into the air, with just his mind."

"Even more if he gets mad," said Fluffy. "I saw him lift two big trucks! Bernard has created a Telepathy Amplifier that can amplify and receive telepathic communications from the other side of the world. Maybe we can use that model to design a Telekinesis Amplifier."

"I'd sure like to see that," said Hacker.

"Hacker is a brilliant engineer and inventor in his own right," said Fluffy. "How long did you say we have, Dr. Handler?"

"Twenty-five days. Assuming it continues at the present rate, impact should take place on July second."

"Then we haven't got a moment to lose," said Bernard.

And, as the team set to work, Laura was busy making a video record of everything with her handheld. She was about to launch her career as a news reporter with the biggest scoop in history.

"I think I should take Mitzi and her babies to the infirmary for a checkup and then to the mouse nursery," said Mama Angelica.

"Mind if I come along?" said Hacker.

"Of course not. It won't take long. I have a new scanning device that will tell us if any of the babies or Mitzi have any health issues in seconds."

"If you'll excuse me, folks, I'll be back soon. Don't make any rash decisions without me," said Hacker. He got into the shoebox with his family, and Mama Angelica took them away.

Caramel was tasked with showing everyone to their rooms. Riordan, Indira, Art, and Laura were given nice guest quarters in the main house.

Realizing they could not contribute anything to the Invention Team, Indira and Riordan stayed in their room. The minute the door closed, she gave him a big kiss. "What was that for?" said Riordan.

"Does it have to be for something?"

"No, but I know it was for something."

"It was for being right. You had a hunch, and you were right. Whether or not all this will be successful remains to be seen, but the fact is, you had a hunch, we took a chance, and—even if we fail—we can go out knowing we tried our best."

"And if we do go out, I for one will go out in love," said Riordan.

"I for two," she said. They kissed again.

"Hey, I was wondering..." said Riordan.

"Yes?"

"Would it be alright with you if Fluffy stayed here with us tonight? I mean, if it's alright with the school."

"And Fluffy. How 'bout if I ask. I'm a stranger to her, and I'd like to get her approval."

So, they went back downstairs to see if Mama Angelica had returned. She was just getting back. She took Hacker out of her pocket and gently set him down on the meeting table, where the ideas were already flying fast and furious. "What did I miss?" said Hacker. "Somebody bring me up to speed!"

Indira pulled Mama Angelica aside and asked if Fluffy could stay with them in their room. "Did you ask Fluffy?" said Mama Angelica.

"Not yet," said Indira. "I wanted to make sure it was alright with you."

"It's alright with me if it's alright with her."

Indira went over to Fluffy and whispered, "Fluffy, your dad and I would like it if you would stay with us in our room tonight."

At first, Fluffy was hesitant and surprised. She still wasn't certain how she felt about this new liaison. She looked over at Mama Angelica, and she gave a subtle nod of approval. Indira seemed so sweet and kind, and the fact that she had been the one to ask made a big impression on Fluffy. "Okay," she said.

That night, Fluffy slept in the bed between Riordan and Indira. She had almost forgotten how much she loved being petted and purring, and she rejoiced at once again being able to snuggle up into her dad's armpit. And Indira didn't smell so bad either. They slept happily and peacefully, each somehow knowing that love goes on, even as worlds end.

Jeremiah Epps was given his own guest room. There was no lock on the door. He could have tried to escape, but that's not what he wanted to do. *They trust me! I wonder why...* Without his accustomed euphorium nightcap, he couldn't fall asleep. A thousand errant thoughts raced through his brain. His mind flashed back to the inciting incident, the cat scratching out his eye. Was it the cat's fault? No, it was his. He was torturing the poor creature, and it was just defending itself. Was it the fault if the GABs that they were as smart and smarter than humans? No, they were the product of human tinkering. *Our fault*, he thought, *and perhaps our good fortune*. After what he had seen today, he searched his heart for the hatred that he had always felt for these animals, and he could not find it. At last, he got up and went downstairs. The Invention Team had decided to keep working through the night, and Epps asked if he could sit in. Perhaps he could be of some assistance. He was given a place at the table. Bernard was demonstrating his Telepathy Amplifier.

"Dr. Van Dusen uses crystals to heal," Bernard was saying, "so I borrowed one— a Clear Quartz Cathedral Crystal, to be exact—and found that it amplified my thoughts when I looked through it. So this crystal is at the heart of my invention. I wonder how it would work with telekinesis...?"

As the sleepy members of the Epsilon upper management team straggled into Meeting Room A, Valerie called the meeting to order, apologized for the late hour and the short notice. She filled them in on what has transpired: Epps's kidnapping, his astronomer hostages and, the final bombshell, the asteroid. Everyone sat in stunned silence. No one complained about being dragged out of bed in the dead of night. Valerie laid out the escape plan and assigned Aurora, who supervised the IT Department, the job of creating a database of the 10,000 most likely candidates in the Western Hemisphere to be included in the evacuation. Epsilon employees were given preference, but other factors were included, such as race and ethnicity, national origin, areas of expertise, and age. It was important that there be a balance of the best minds and bodies in the creative arts and athletics, as well as tech. It was also important to take a lot of children and young adults, as they would be the hope of perpetuating the human race. "Today is June seventh—almost June eighth," she said. "It is imperative that the list be complete and all the invitations sent out by June eighteenth. On June twenty-eighth we all leave for Huston and from there take shuttles to Moonbase, where the interstellar spacecraft Epsilon is waiting for us. We cast off for Gliese on July first."

Anyone who thought that this would be a fair and impartial process by a fair and impartial computer was delusional. Aurora Malvolio-Jones became the most powerful (and popular) person on Earth overnight. The news about the impending doom spread far and wide after the meeting, and everyone was petitioning Aurora for a spot on the ship.

Aurora herself was in a quandary: Should she take her husband or her boyfriend—or both? Of course, Valerie slipped Aurora quite a long a list of people she wanted included, and this was not negotiable. There was a no pets rule because there were no cryogenic pods provided for animals, and some people actually chose to stay and die rather than go without their pets.

The computer program they designed to choose candidates outside of Epsilon was also flawed. For instance, it thought having a baseball team would be a good idea, so it picked a kind of all-star team: the top players in each position who had the highest stats, and, of course, the winningest coach and manager (who, it turned out, had worked together on another team and who were sworn enemies). The only problem was that it forgot to pick another team for the all-stars to play.

Not only that, but the gravity on Gliese being nearly twice that of Earth would make a baseball as heavy as a brick, and a bat like a lead pipe. The same blunder was made with basketball, football, and soccer, none of which would be playable on Gliese 667 Cc.

At Animal U, an emergency meeting of all students and staff was called for ten o'clock the next morning. As everyone filed into the Great Hall, the Invention Team—Bernard, Hacker, Dr. Handler, Dr. Messner, and Jeremiah Epps—had been up all night sketching out possible plans for the device and how to bring together the maximum number of telekinetic animals and people to help deflect the asteroid. Dr. Handler repeated the demonstration of the night before, showing the entire community the horrific image of the asteroid coming toward them.

Bernard addressed the room: "We now have only twenty-four days before this thing destroys our planet. Unless we can stop it. We—all of you and all telekinetic beings around the world—are the only hope we have. You've all seen my Telepathy Amplifier. We've been exploring the idea of building a similar device, only one that amplifies Telekinesis—and much bigger. The idea is if we can all concentrate our telekinetic powers on changing the asteroid's trajectory in exactly the same way at exactly the same moment, and if we can build a device to project all that power into space and focus it on that object, we just might have a chance. The Invention Team—Dr. Handler, Dr. Messner, Hacker, Mr. Epps, and myself—will work day and night to come up with the plans and a list of materials we will need. Many things will have to be brought in from the outside world, and we can no longer afford to worry about keeping Animal U a secret. Mr. Epps has offered to use his own resources to procure the parts we will need for our invention." A murmur of surprised approval rose from the crowd. "In a few days, I will use the Telepathy Amplifier to invite all telekinetic beings who can travel to come to Animal U and help us. It will be the greatest and riskiest experiment of all time, but what have we got to lose, right?"

The crowd expressed its approval in various ways: those with hands clapped, the rest meowed, barked, oinked and squeaked to raise the roof.

After the meeting, Fluffy asked Riordan and Indira to come with her. "I have someone I want you to meet," she told Riordan. She took them to where Jack and Sally lived. "Dad, this is my brother Jack and his wife Sally."

"So you found him! Hello, Jack, I'm Jim. Hello, Sally."

Jack and Sally activated their tablets so they could speak audibly. "Hello, Jim," said Jack. "You did a fine job of raising my sister. She's the smartest and bravest cat I've ever known."

"In two months Sally will be having kittens," said Fluffy, "the first new generation of GABs from our freshman..." She cut herself short, remembering the impending doom, and wished she hadn't spoken.

Riordan and Indira congratulated the happy couple. "Jack, I want to apologize," said Riordan.

"What do you mean?" said Jack.

"When I got Fluffy five years ago, I left you. You were the last kitten left. I should have taken you as well. Your life would have been much better if I had."

"I don't blame you, Jim. None of us can know the future, and my life is wonderful now, so all's well that ends well, right?"

"That is if we can stop the world from ending," said Sally, a little tremor in her voice.

Jack looked at her adoringly. "Even if it does, I wouldn't have it any other way."

CHAPTER FOURTEEN — END TIMES

It was inevitable after the meeting at Epsilon that the news of the end of the world would leak out. Saturday afternoon CNS carried a special bulletin citing rumors of an asteroid headed for Earth and a mass evacuation of the elite cons. Dr. Stephen Boyd of the Harvard Physics department was interviewed about the disappearance of all the important astronomers and the closing of all the world's observatories. He speculated that the rumors of an asteroid approaching Earth were likely true. But no one had conclusive proof. "No one we can find, anyway."

When the rank and file employees at Epsilon, the police, the fire department, and Animal Control learned that they would not be evacuated with their elite bosses, they walked off the job, preferring to spend what time remained at home with their families. Epsilon sent everyone home and closed its doors. At the animal detention centers, all the animals were set free. Chaos broke out on the streets, with gangs of young rips looting and burning the structures of the rich.

The same day, Bernard sent out his worldwide announcement through his Telepathy Amplifier.

Within a few hours, Route 28 became a steady stream of animals walking up West Kill Mountain. Soon the road was also jammed with cars full of panicked families and even people on foot who had poured out of the ripcoms to escape the riots. The city had become very dangerous with no police on the job.

In spite of the doomsday rumors, Chief Davis was intent on finding Epps. He had interviewed both Hobson and Valerie, and he was convinced they were hiding something from him.

As soon as Zvonar picked up Bernard's broadcast, he went immediately to Davis. "It was an amplified telepathic transmission from a place called Animal U on West Kill Mountain. It was from a big dog. He said an asteroid was going to destroy the Earth and he invited all animals to go up there and help them try to move it off course using telekinesis."

"I'll bet that's where they've taken Epps," said Davis.

"It is. I'm sure of it," said Zvonar.

An hour later, Davis, Zvonar, and four armed troopers in full battle gear were in a gunship looking down at the unusually heavy traffic on Route 28.

At Animal U construction of the device was already underway. Earlier in the day, two cargo copters from Epsilon factories had delivered the aluminum alloy and tungsten parts the Invention Team had ordered, along with boxes of small electronic components, hardware, and ten perfect Clear Quartz Cathedral Crystals. Now all the animals were putting the parts together on the grassy quad. There were two large parabolic dishes. One would be the projection dish and would be aimed skyward, with a wand in the center that would direct the concentrated beam of telekinetic energy at the target. The other was erected atop a sturdy girder and was turned downward, like a giant umbrella. All the animals would gather under the umbrella which, simply put, would suck up their telekinetic power and transmit it to the projection dish. Under the umbrella, attached to the center post, would be four large video monitors, aimed north, south, east and west, which would display the view from the Galileo to the gathered participants. Hacker and a team of precision mouse engineers were working on the fine circuitry that would be the guts of the control consul.

The sound of the approaching gunship made everyone stop and look to the west. Fluffy was working with Jack, Sally, Riordan, and Indira. Hearing the war copter reminded her of that awful day Fang had died and she had killed the unmanned drone. As the copter came into view, she wondered what she would do if they opened fire. There were people in this one. Hacker, who was on a big work table with his team, called to Mama Angelica: "Should we knock it down?"

"No," she said calmly, "let them come."

"I know who it is," said Epps. "Let me handle this."

The copter landed twenty yards off, in the center of the great quad. The four troopers, assault weapons in hand, leaped out as soon as the door opened and nervously formed a defensive semi-circle, weapons trained on the animals and people on the quad. Davis and Zvonar descended and surveyed the situation for a moment. Then Epps came forward, striding confidently across the lawn to meet them.

"You don't need your guns here, Chief," said Epps. Davis had his men lower their weapons.

"We've come to take you out of here, sir," said Davis. "Come with us and join the evacuation."

"I'm not going," said Epps.

"What do you mean?"

"Just that. I'm staying here."

"You really think these animals can stop the asteroid with their thoughts?" Davis chuckles. Zvonar does not.

"I'm betting my life on it. Listen, Davis, I was wrong about these animals. I've been wrong about a lot of things. But I see clearly now. You and your men are welcome to stay here and help us, or you can go home and pack. But I'm staying here."

"I'm gonna be awful pissed off if you're right," said Davis, smiling. "I have to admit, there's something about this place that kind of knocks the wind out of your sails."

The two men shook hands. Then Davis motioned everyone back into the gunship and they took off for home.

Epps returned to work as if nothing had happened. Mama Angelica, Fluffy and Bernard exchanged looks and smiles, as if to say: "See, no one is beyond redemption."

From out of the bowels of West Kill Mountain, the first new arrivals began to file down the dirt path toward the campus. Mama Angelica told the kitchen crew to make extra rations; the population at Animal U was about to double.

CHAPTER FIFTEEN — THE FINAL PUSH

The people and animals worked day and night for ten days. On Tuesday, June nineteenth, the Telekinesis Amplifier was ready to be tested. Dr. Handler was at the control console. He wore a headset with earphones and a mic which enabled him to communicate, not only with the circle of animals here but also with the three other Animal U's around the world who had also built Telekinesis Amplifiers. The test target was a small asteroid, fifteen million miles out in space. He trained the Galileo on the object and magnified the image until it looked nearly as menacing as the giant rock that was almost at their doorstep. All the animals at Animal U who could fit gathered under the giant umbrella; others clustered around the edges. Every eye was fixed on one of the monitors. Dr. Handler placed a small white arrow on the screens to the right of the object, pointing to the left. There was another arrow to the left of the object. He addressed the crowd over a P.A. "When I say 'now,' everyone concentrate on moving the object to the left, all the way to the left arrow. Ready? Commencing countdown..." He counted backward from ten to zero and said "NOW." Silently, everyone focused their energy. The asteroid did not move. The Invention Team huddled. "We have to go over the plans and all the circuitry again," said Handler, shaking his head.

"Either we need to increase the power, or there's a glitch somewhere," said Hacker.

Bernard addressed the crowd: "Don't lose heart, everyone. Obviously, we need to figure out and fix the problem. We still have a little time. Give us a few days, and we'll do another test."

Over the next ten days, the Invention Team disassembled the Telekinetic Amplifier, painstakingly tested every component, and put it back together. Everything seemed to be in order.

Laura interviewed the Invention Team for CNS, recording everything on her handheld for later broadcast. She had decided not to release any of the footage unless and until the disaster had been averted. There was no sense in getting the world's hopes up if the experiment was a failure.

On Friday, June thirtieth, they scheduled another test. "There is nothing wrong with the device," said Dr. Handler. "The problem is we were not able to generate enough force. We're out of time. This time, we have to deflect the asteroid that's coming toward us."

Once again, all the animals at Animal U and around the world were assembled beneath the big umbrella. Bernard made sure Fluffy—his prize student—was in the front row, near the center of the circle. Pandora was a few rows back. Dr. Handler brought up the image of the giant rock on the monitors. There was dead silence, as everyone gathered all their concentration, all their strength. Dr. Handler commenced the countdown. When Handler said "Now," everyone concentrated on moving the object to the left. It didn't move. It just kept coming. A deathly pall fell over the crowd.

Fluffy asked to speak with the Invention Team. "I don't pretend to know anything about these things," she said. "Maybe it was a science program I saw on TV when I was young, but I was thinking..."

"Yes?" they all said as one.

"Well, maybe we could slow the asteroid down by pushing it back, instead of to one side..."

"Yes," said Dr. Messner excitedly, "if we can slow it down—even a little—its trajectory and the Earth's will no longer intersect, and it will miss us."

And so, they decided to try pushing the asteroid back to make it slow down. Everyone was quite exhausted, so it was decided to go for the final push bright and early the next morning. The next day was July first; the day before the asteroid was scheduled to hit.

Everyone dispersed and went back to their dorms. Fluffy went with Riordan and Indira to sleep in the main house, but few got much sleep that night.

Very early the next morning, Fluffy was awakened by the buzzing of her tablet. It was an urgent message from Pandora: "Fluffy, I need to show you something important. Meet me in room 321 in the main house in 20 minutes."

Room 321 was a small, rarely-used classroom on the third floor of the main house. Indira and her dad were still asleep, so Fluffy silently left the room and went upstairs to room 321. It smelled musty and old in there and, indeed, the building itself was more than 300 years old. Van Dusen Manor had been built in 1774. The architecture was in the neo-gothic style of a grand English manor house. Fluffy thought it looked like Manderley in Hitchcock's *Rebecca*.

She entered the silent room and, the moment she did, the door slammed shut behind her. She heard a key turn in the lock. She was locked in. "Pandora? Pandora, this isn't funny. We have to be on the quad in a few minutes!" But there was no answer from Pandora. Fluffy looked around the room. There were old wooden desks lined up in front of the teacher's desk, a blackboard. It was a typical old-fashioned classroom. She leaped up onto the radiator and then the window sill and looked out. She was looking down at the quad. The animals and people were beginning to assemble for the final push—to put Fluffy's theory to the test. She tried to get the window to open, but it was jammed shut. She looked for something she could use to pick the lock on the door, a paper clip maybe, but she could find nothing.

Below on the quad, Bernard and the others were looking and calling for Fluffy. "She is my strongest student," said Bernard. "Not having her in the circle could make the difference between success and failure." Meanwhile, Pandora had moved up closer to the center of the circle and now occupied Fluffy's place. Bernard scrutinized her. "Pandora, do you know where Fluffy is?"

"No, I have no idea. But I'll do my best to take her place."

At that very moment, Fluffy was trying to contact Bernard telepathically but was getting so much cross-talk from the gathered throng, she couldn't train in on his frequency.

Desperate, Fluffy picked up a desk and, with all her telekinetic might, flung it against the door. But the ancient solid oak door did not budge. Then she thought of throwing something through the window, but she was afraid it might land on somebody below. She searched through the drawers of the teacher's desk, which had been purchased a long time ago at a secondhand store, and at last found a marble. A tiny marble some teacher had confiscated from some little kid centuries ago. This would be tricky. She had to fling the marble through one of the panes of leaded glass, but not let it fall to the ground. She hurled it and broke the glass nearest the window sill. Then she snatched it back through the hole it had made. She did this twice more until there was a hole in the glass big enough for her to crawl through.

"I appreciate the thought, Pandora," Bernard was saying, "but we really need Fluffy for this."

Pandora seethed inside, but she remained outwardly calm.

A hundred feet above them, Fluffy crawled out onto the outer window sill, then cautiously along the ornate stonework of the building's façade, clinging to gargoyles and finials. "Hey!" she shouted, hoping someone would hear her below. Then louder: "Helloooo down there!"

At last, Bernard looked up. "My god, it's Fluffy!" he shouted. The others looked up and saw her.

Riordan was terrified. "How do we get her down?"

"Get the golf cart," cried Mama Angelica.

Riordan got the concept instantly. He ran for the little golf cart with the canvas roof. He drove it right up against the façade of the building and right below where Fluffy was perched. "Fluffy, do you think you can jump onto the canvas?" he called.

"I think so," she said. And not wanting to give it too much thought, she took the leap. A hundred feet below, she came crashing through the canvas roof and landed in the cushioned back seat of the golf cart, miraculously unhurt.

"Hurry, there's no time to lose," said Handler.

In her penthouse apartment, not far from Riordan's place in Kingston, Valerie Trump was frantic. By her own decree, she was not allowed to take more than two hundred pounds of belongings. What should she take, and—more importantly—what should she leave behind? She had boxes of precious jewels, but what good would they do her on Gliese 667 Cc? By all accounts, it was a cold, dark planet with more gravity, less light, and thinner air than Earth. It would be like life on the old frontier. Maybe she should just take her camping clothes. She might have to live in a makeshift shelter for years until proper residences were constructed. And what about all her gorgeous furniture and art pieces? She really wanted her beautiful things around her in this strange new world, but they would surely exceed the weight limit. And where would she hide 600 pairs of shoes?

She had her faithful manservant, Rusty, an anatomically correct tenth-generation Epsilon Android, Model 324M (the M was for male), crate everything up and mark it SCIENTIFIC INSTRUMENTS. Since Rusty would not need a sleep pod, Valerie had arranged for him to accompany her on the voyage. What the hell. What was the point of being the most powerful person on Earth if you couldn't bend the rules occasionally? "Note to self," she muttered, "lay in a good supply of euphorium, and the means to make more."

On Thursday, June twenty-eighth, pandemonium reigned at Kingston Airport, as thousands of elite cons, all armed with special invitations, poured in from far and wide, all clamoring to board the Electrojets that would take them to the Huston Space Center.

Valerie, Aurora, and the entire Epsilon upper management team traveled together in a stretch limo that carried all seven of them in comfort. But when they alighted at the airport it suddenly became every man for himself, and even the top executives were shoved aside by those with greater size and strength, bent on reaching the boarding gates first. *When push comes to shove—and it seems that it has—humans have not really evolved past the stone age*, thought Valerie. *And this is who I'll be stuck with for the next fifty years...*

The chosen boarded the planes that flew them to Houston Space Center. There, ten moon shuttles made constant trips to Moonbase and back, delivering the evacuees and supplies over a period of three days. By Monday, July first, all of the evacuees were in their pods in a state of cryogenic hibernation and, manned by a robot crew, the starship Epsilon fired up its massive engines and departed for Gliese 667 Cc, henceforth to be known as the planet Epsilon.

At Animal U, Fluffy joined the others in the great circle under the umbrella. Pandora was right beside her. Their eyes met, Fluffy's asking "Why?" Pandora looked away. *I guess humans are not the only ones who do stupid things for stupid reasons*, she thought. But this was not a time for recriminations. Fluffy knew they all had to push together or die.

The Tuareg drummers had been called on to provide a hypnotic rhythm that would enhance the animals' ability to concentrate. As the appointed hour approached, they started their slow, relentless beat. The animals swayed imperceptibly as Handler began the countdown: "Ten, nine, eight, seven, six, five, four, three, two, one, NOW!" They looked intently at the big rock, tumbling end over end on the monitors. "Push it," cried Handler, "push it back!" They pushed on the rock with all their might for five full minutes and still, nothing was happening. At last Dr. Messner cleared his throat over the P.A. "It's slowing," he said. He began to read out the speed: "18,125 miles per hour...18,018 miles per hour...17,908 miles per hour...it's working, keep pushing! 17,887 miles per hour! You did it. The asteroid will miss us!" Everyone cheered. The drum beats got faster, livelier, and soon the somber circle turned into a circle dance, with everyone embracing and dancing for joy. Sally's kittens would be born, Hacker and Mitzi's babies would grow up, and Fluffy could look forward to a life of endless possibilities.

The next day, July second, was to be Doomsday. The sky began to darken, and huge winds began to blow. Tidal waves rose out of the oceans and wiped out seacoast towns. Kingston harbor was heavily damaged. At noon, the animals looked up, and the sky had turned to stone. The giant asteroid was passing right above them. It moved in slow motion, its fearful topography seemed close enough to touch. The howling winds blew stronger and stronger, knocking down trees and tearing roofs off some of the buildings. Everyone huddled together in the Great Hall, which had withstood centuries of inclement weather. Hours passed. Finally, the sky brightened, and the sun shone at Animal U once again.

Laura interviewed Bernard, Hacker, Handler, Messner, and Epps for the final installment of her report to CNS: "Dr. Handler, how close to the Earth did the asteroid pass?"

"We calculate about 300 miles. It just missed the Earth's atmosphere. If it had been any closer, it would have burst into flames and burned up much of our planet."

"Dr. Messner, what were some of the obstacles you had to overcome to make the asteroid miss us?"

"The most important breakthrough, I think, was made by Fluffy here." Indira handed him a reticent Fluffy. Messner cradled her lovingly in his arms. "Without any formal physics training, this brilliant cat figured out that it would be easier for the animals to slow the asteroid down than to push it to one side. But the most amazing thing was the wonderful team effort made by all the telekinetic animals around the world, who pulled together and saved our planet."

Jeremiah Epps cut in. "I – I want to say something... I was responsible for exterminating thousands—maybe hundreds of thousands—of GAB animals. I can never make up for that sin. Yet, these animals and people here at Animal U welcomed me with no malice, no hatred in their hearts." He teared up, dabbed his bad eye with a handkerchief. "I was wrong—terribly wrong—about the GABs, about a lot of things. We have a lot of rebuilding and rethinking to do. If I'm a part of that, I want the GABs included in planning our new world. They have so much to teach us."

"For CNS, this is Laura Larson reporting from Animal U somewhere in the Catskill Mountains." Laura edited together all the footage she had amassed and sent it on to CNS. The next morning, Laura was all over every TV screen on Earth.

"What will you do now, Fluffy?" asked Riordan. He searched her face for some hint of human expression. "Indira and I were hoping you would come home and live with us. We could be a family."

"I would love that, Dad. But at least for now, I think my place is here. There's so much work to be done building the new world, and this is where it starts. But I can come home for holidays. Will you both be living in the penthouse in Kingston?"

"No. I've decided to give that to Art and Laura—if it's still there. The light there is very good for painting. I'm going to move into Indira's little place in Cambridge. From the first moment I arrived there, I felt that place was my home."

"I can't wait to see it," said Fluffy. "Cats love cozy places."

The next day, Riordan, Indira, Handler, Art, and Laura said their goodbyes and made their way up the dirt path to the tunnel through West Kill Mountain. As they emerged through the falls on the other side and climbed up the west bank to the footbridge, they were somewhat surprised to see Art's van, still parked in the same place, unscathed.

"Oh," said Art, "I almost forgot, professor..." He opened the back door of the van and pulled out a canvas wrapped in cloth. He unwrapped it and presented it to Riordan. It was the portrait of Fluffy, abstract, colors blazing, but clearly her: the pink nose, the whiskers, the white face peaking in a star point, and those green eyes, shining with intelligence and curiosity.

"It's perfect, Art. Just as I imagined it. Thank you."

Epps stayed behind at Animal U. A few days later a helicopter would come and take him home, but he wanted to stay and help with the rebuilding. "You're welcome to stay as long as you like," said Mama Angelica.

"Don't worry, I'll be back. I want to help you build this school into a full-fledged university. If that's what you want."

"It is," said Bernard.

And so it was that Animal U became the first seat of learning to integrate GABs and humans in the faculty and the student body. And this became the first building block of the new world.

ABOUT THE AUTHOR

After twenty years trembling on the brink of rock stardom and fifteen years working at record companies, Ted Myers left the music business—or perhaps it was the other way around—and took a job as a copywriter at an advertising agency. This cemented his determination to make his mark as an author. Among his many publications are: *Making It: Music, Sex & Drugs in the Golden Age of Rock* (Calumet Editions, 2017) and many short stories in anthologies and literary magazines.

Thank you so much for reading one of our **Sci-Fi** novels.
If you enjoyed our book, please check out our recommended title for your
next great read!

Culture-Z by Karl Andrew Marszalowicz

In the year 2190, mankind has made great strides forward in the worlds of
technology, science, and greed. However, when all three get together one
last time, this oblivious generation may not exist much longer.

Lightning Source UK Ltd.
Milton Keynes UK
UKHW010650280319
340056UK00001B/165/P